Praise for Jon Mayhew

MONSTER ODYSSEY

'Rip-roaring, page-turning adventure'
Books for Keeps

'Full of heart-stopping moments that will have you
on the edge of your seat'
Primary Times

'A rip-roaring gung-ho adventure'
Financial Times

'History and fantasy collide in this breathlessly
paced adventure'
Bookseller

MORTLOCK

Shortlisted for the Waterstones Children's Book Prize

'A macabre, darkly humorous adventure peppered with
deadly thrills. A dazzling debut'
Guardian

'Mortlock is a thrilling adventure from start to finish'
SciFi Now

'Mayhew has woven a rich tapestry depicting a series of
convincing worlds'
Observer

Also by Jon Mayhew

Monster Odyssey – The Eye of Neptune
Monster Odyssey – The Wrath of the Lizard Lord
Monster Odyssey – The Curse of the Ice Serpent

Mortlock
The Demon Collector
The Bonehill Curse

THE VENOM
OF THE
SCORPION

JON MAYHEW

BLOOMSBURY
LONDON OXFORD NEW YORK NEW DELHI SYDNEY

Bloomsbury Publishing, London, Oxford, New York, New Delhi and Sydney

First published in Great Britain in January 2016 by Bloomsbury Publishing Plc
50 Bedford Square, London WC1B 3DP

www.bloomsbury.com
www.JonMayhewBooks.com

Bloomsbury is a registered trademark of Bloomsbury Publishing Plc

A CIP catalogue record for this book is available from the British Library

ISBN 978 1 4088 5425 9

Typeset by RefineCatch Limited, Bungay, Suffolk
Printed and bound in Great Britain by CPI Group (UK) Ltd, Croydon CR0 4YY

1 3 5 7 9 10 8 6 4 2

'The horrid scowl with which he died was fixed on his features. Having lived but for vengeance, his hate still survived.'

Jules Verne, *The Steam House*

CORNWALL,
1816

CHAPTER ONE
PIRATES

Dakkar clung to the knotted rope that stretched up the stern of the pirate ship. His hands felt numb with the cold and damp and his world rocked about on the rolling waves, making it hard to keep climbing.

'Why can't we just ram this bloomin' wreck and sink her?' Fletcher hissed behind him. Fletcher was Dakkar's friend, a cabin boy who often fought alongside him. The boy gripped his own rope and was struggling as much as Dakkar. His dirty mop of blond hair clung to his wet skin.

'Keep quiet!' Dakkar said through gritted teeth. 'You know we've got to free the prisoners on board.'

Commander Blizzard, their leader, had brought them to this place after a pirate ship had been spotted. The pirates weren't after gold, though; they were after slaves. A whole village of men, women and children had been taken from the Cornish coast. Dakkar and Fletcher had to rescue them.

Dakkar inched his way up the rope, his feet pressing against the wet planks. Above him, a dim light glowed from some small windows, probably the captain's cabin. The Barbary pirate ship was an old girl, taken years ago but crewed by tough sailors from North Africa. Dakkar found it hard to believe that these men would travel so far to take people for slavery, but here they were. Commander Blizzard had told him that raids as far north as Iceland had been known.

A comet of light jerked Dakkar from his thoughts as a cannonball arced from the darkness, turning the night lurid red.

'Come on!' Dakkar snapped. 'The commander's started firing. We should have those prisoners out of the ship by now!' He dragged himself up the rope, hand over hand, until his shoulders and arms ached.

'Wait for me!' Fletcher called after him.

Shouts echoed across the ship, underscored by the stamp and thud of feet on deck, as men ran to ready the cannon for battle. Dakkar came to the rear window and glanced inside to see a sumptuous cabin, strewn with furs and rich fabrics. Golden goblets sat on the table and charts lay spread across the room. Otherwise it was empty. Dakkar grinned. 'Let's go in through here,' he said.

Another boom from the cannon on Commander Blizzard's ship, HMS *Slaughter*, told him to get a move on. 'They'll hit their target any minute and then things will get interesting.' Dakkar kicked hard against the stern of the pirate ship with both feet and swung away from it.

Then he came swinging back, putting both feet through the window.

Offering a silent prayer of thanks for his thick boots and tough canvas trousers, Dakkar crashed through the glass and landed on his feet in the middle of the cabin. Fletcher clambered in after him.

'Blimey, Dakkar, no need to make such an entrance.'

'We can't waste time.' Dakkar grinned. 'This is the most direct route.'

'You're the boss.' Fletcher smiled. 'Beat you to the door!'

They both glanced at each other then raced for the cabin door. But it swung open itself, helped by a huge bald man with a long drooping moustache. A scorpion tattoo on the man's bare arm seemed to move whenever he flexed his iron muscles. He stared down at Dakkar and Fletcher with a creased brow, as if trying to work out where these two boys had sprung from. Dakkar didn't give him a chance to speak but jabbed him sharply in the stomach with his fist. The man doubled up and Fletcher brought both his hands down on the back of the man's neck. The pirate crumpled to the ground.

'Finished him off for you,' Fletcher panted, jumping over the body and out of the door.

'I could have dealt with him alone!' Dakkar called and then slipped out after him.

Fire raged on the deck where a third cannonball had hit a powder keg. Men scurried about, readying cannon, but a large crowd pushed a capstan, a huge block of wood with handles sticking out of it; the capstan wound up chains and winched up anchors. The men yelled urgently in Turkish to each other. A loud, metal, grating sound screeched through the air.

'Are they getting ready to leave?' Dakkar frowned. 'Or winching something up from the bottom?'

'Never mind that,' Fletcher yelled. 'Come on before we're spotted!'

Dakkar hurried to a huge square grate that sat in the centre of the deck. The ship was quite small and this hatch led to the hold where the prisoners were kept.

He gripped the metal grille and yanked it aside. The dank smell of the sea and unwashed bodies drifted up and he peered into the shadows to see frightened faces of men, women and children staring up at him.

'It's all right,' Fletcher said over his shoulder. 'Mr Fletcher, His Majesty's Navy!'

Dakkar gave him a sidelong glance and extended a hand. 'Come on, follow us. We have a rescue boat at the back of the ship!'

Another explosion rocked the deck and Dakkar nearly plunged headlong into the hold. The prisoners looked fearfully at him.

'Don't be afraid,' Fletcher said, grinning. 'He's one of us! Now come on!'

A woman began scrambling up the steps out of the hold and quickly others followed. They looked ragged and bruised by their ordeal. But Dakkar was still taking in Fletcher's comment.

'One of . . . ?' Dakkar stared in disbelief.

A cry distracted him and he turned to see one of the pirates pointing at them. Dakkar pulled his pistol and shot the man in the kneecap. But others turned now and drew their swords.

'Get them to safety. I'll keep these men occupied,' Dakkar said, bundling Fletcher towards the stern.

'Aye, aye, sir,' Fletcher said.

Dakkar grinned and pulled out a pouch of powder from his pocket. Dakkar had lived with a man called Franciszek Oginski for many years and the man had taught him many things, including how to design ingenious weapons that helped make escape possible. 'Get going!' He hurled the pouch in front of the approaching men and it exploded in a choking cloud of smoke. Dakkar launched into the fog, stabbing one man in the arm and kicking another's legs from under him.

Another cannonball buzzed over his head and crashed into the mainmast, sending splinters of wood across the deck. The mainsail drifted down like a blanket over them all. Dakkar punched the heavy canvas away and rolled from under it.

He thumped the hilt of his sword into the three heads he could see under the sail and then backed away, following Fletcher and the retreating prisoners.

Fire had taken hold of the pirate ship now, and the crew that remained hurried to douse the flames or were trying to return fire on HMS *Slaughter* with the cannon. The capstan lay abandoned and a tall, bare-chested man with his hair tied in a topknot strode towards Dakkar, swinging a curved scimitar. Dakkar shivered. The scimitar was a hacking blade, like a butcher's cleaver. It would slice through flesh and splinter bone with ease. The man's muscled body gleamed in the firelight as he made a few practice strokes through the air.

Dakkar kicked a small barrel towards him, hoping to trip him up, but the man easily sidestepped it with a smirk. He was close now; Dakkar could smell the stale sweat on his body and see a glint of gold in his yellowed teeth. He swung the blade, forcing Dakkar to throw himself backward. The scimitar hummed above Dakkar's head. The man gave a grin and raised the blade high. In that fleeting moment, Dakkar noticed a scorpion tattoo on the man's arm. *Another one*, he thought, then turned his attention to survival.

More explosions rocked the ship and the deck tilted, sending the man stumbling away for a second. Dakkar leapt to his feet. The cabin door was open behind him and he could see the prisoners climbing down the cargo net that Fletcher had brought up to enable them all to escape.

If Dakkar joined them, the man would likely follow and probably cut the ropes holding the net. He turned and raised his sword.

The man saw his predicament and climbed to his feet, stumbling back across the angled deck towards him. He swung the sword and Dakkar parried the blow. Sparks flared off his blade and the shock ran up his arm, numbing his muscles. Dakkar hissed with pain and fell on to the deck.

'You die now, boy.' The man grinned. He straddled Dakkar's body and raised the sword with both hands.

Instinctively, Dakkar kicked upward, catching the man between his legs with a powerful blow. The man gasped and dropped the blade, swinging his hands down in a pointless attempt to defend himself. He doubled up, groaning in agony. It would have been comical if the ship hadn't given another lurch, sending Dakkar and the man sliding to the starboard side of the ship.

'We're sinking, Fletcher. Is everyone on the *Nautilus*?'

The *Nautilus*, Dakkar's submarine, waited directly behind the pirate ship and Fletcher guided them down the stern of the ship on to its deck.

'Just a few more!' Fletcher yelled back.

Dakkar turned and began to climb the steep incline that had once been a level deck. Barrels and boxes bounced past him into the encroaching sea.

Then the water exploded and a huge shrieking roar split the air. Dakkar rolled on to his back, pressing himself against the deck, and stared at a huge pair of yellow eyes, glowering from a head the size of a carriage. The only other thing Dakkar could see was row upon row of razor-sharp teeth and a blood-red jaw opening wide to engulf him.

CHAPTER TWO
SEA BEAST

The creature reared up, its long neck snaking out of the foaming water that splashed against the tilting deck.

'Now, what on earth are you doing here?' Dakkar muttered and scrambled backward, crab-like, towards the cabin door.

Ever since Dakkar had become entangled in Franciszek Oginski's battle with the evil organisation known as Cryptos, he'd faced all kinds of fearsome beasts and monsters. Cryptos was run by Oginski's six evil brothers and they delighted in using terrifying creatures and ingenious machines to further their evil plans.

The long-neck snapped at him, narrowly missing his boots. The smell of rotten fish and the sea washed over Dakkar. He glanced around for a weapon and saw the scimitar glimmering in the light of the fire that blazed about them.

Once more the creature shrieked and bit down at

Dakkar. With a yell, Dakkar rolled and snatched up the scimitar. He sliced down, gripping the sword with both hands. The steel bit into flesh and a loud shriek rewarded Dakkar as the snout pulled back. At first, Dakkar had thought it was some kind of sea serpent, but now he saw a muscular body and broad flippers behind the snake-like neck.

The monster slapped a massive flipper on to the deck, hauling itself after him and sending the ship lurching downward into the sea. Water rushed up the deck towards Dakkar and he lost his footing. The creature's head snaked behind him and bit at his neck but Dakkar whirled the blade round, the steel grating on sharp teeth.

Seawater swirled round Dakkar's knees. Barrels and boxes and bodies floated everywhere, thumping into each other in the boiling water. Dakkar could feel the pull of the sea on his legs and the creature had dragged more of its huge bulk on to the deck. He glanced at the rear cabin door but the water poured in through it, making that exit impossible. *I just hope Fletcher got everybody out in time*, he thought.

Panting for breath, Dakkar waded towards the quarter-deck at the stern of the ship, above the flooded rear cabin where Fletcher had been.

The beast shrieked again and Dakkar cut an arc through the air with the butcher's blade. This time it crunched into the side of the long-neck's head, carving a deep, bloody furrow in the slimy skin.

The creature backed off and reared up high above Dakkar. He stood on the steps that led to the rear deck, facing the monster and holding the scimitar with a weakening grip. He was in a terrible position and exhaustion was beginning to take hold of his body.

This is it, he thought. *I'm going to die.*

Then suddenly a loud buzz filled the air, followed by a distant muffled boom, and the monster's head vanished in an explosion of blood and brain. Dakkar's vision blurred and faded and he thought he heard distant cheering. The lifeless neck slapped down, smashing timbers and throwing up a tidal wave of bloody water.

With legs like wet paper, Dakkar staggered up the steps on to the rear deck, closely followed by the rising water. The ship was sinking fast now and the bitter cold sea gnawed into Dakkar's thighs, then his waist, making him gasp. The water boiled and hissed as it doused the burning wreck. He looked up and saw another huge shape blot out the night sky.

'I've got him, Georgia.' Fletcher's voice sounded distant but a firm hand caught Dakkar's collar. 'I tell you, this boy's becoming a liability.'

Dakkar felt himself being lifted on to the deck of the *Nautilus*. He could feel its snug-fitted boards, the polished wood and the slightly rounded surface. He shook his head and coughed up a gutful of bloody seawater.

'Thank you, Fletcher,' he said, clambering to his feet and falling down almost straight away. 'I'll be fine now.'

A crowd of prisoners huddled on the deck, staring at him warily.

'You don't look fine.' Fletcher grinned. 'You look a mess! And what have you clung on to that for?'

Dakkar looked down. He was still holding the scimitar in his hand. It felt good, though, heavy and powerful. 'Well, I did win it fair and square.'

'Come on, let's get you inside,' Fletcher said.

They stood at the front of the *Nautilus*, which was, in effect, a streamlined wooden tube with a tower set in the middle. The crowd on the deck stepped back as Dakkar approached, some of them preferring to almost fall into the sea than to touch Dakkar.

'What's wrong with you all?' Dakkar snarled at the nearest woman. 'Have I grown an extra head or something?'

'Beggin' your pardon, sir,' the woman said, trying an awkward curtsy. 'We thought you was one of them.' She gave a nod to the water, indicating where the last traces of the pirate ship bubbled to the bottom of the sea and a dead pirate rocked, face down in the water.

'Thought I was a pirate?' Dakkar frowned, dumbfounded.

'It's your dark looks, and that sword doesn't help things along.' Fletcher nodded at his scimitar.

'Nonsense.' Dakkar barged past them, climbing the tower to get inside. 'I'm Prince of Bundelkhand in India, not some North African pirate! You're lucky I came to save you. I wonder if you deserve it at all now.'

The warmth of the *Nautilus* soaked into his bones as he climbed down the inside of the tower and into the control room at its base. Georgia sat in the captain's chair, a wheel in front of her and various levers, dials and switches surrounding her. She smiled as Dakkar came down the ladder. Georgia Fulton and Dakkar had been firm friends since their first adventure, when they had to rescue Franciszek Oginski and her uncle, the American inventor Robert Fulton, from Cryptos two years ago. They'd had many adventures since.

'Managed to find something big and hungry to play with then?' she said, spinning round on the chair. 'What was that critter?'

'Critter?' Dakkar shuddered. 'The way you Americans mangle the English language! Anyway, it's not funny, Georgia. That thing could have killed me and what does it suggest to you?'

'I know: it says Cryptos, loud and clear,' she said with a sigh.

Cryptos was run by the brothers Oginski, seven brothers who had sworn vengeance on the world after their family home was destroyed by a Russian invasion. Franciszek, Dakkar's mentor, had finally turned against his brothers and renounced the evil aims of Cryptos. Sadly, he'd died defending Dakkar.

'How do you know it's Cryptos then?' Fletcher said, joining them from above.

'Only Cryptos has the knowledge and ability to breed these monsters,' Dakkar said. 'That one probably came from the underworld that Stefan Oginski tried to rule. The pirates must have held it in a cage under the boat and released it when they were attacked. Did you see those men at the capstan when HMS *Slaughter* opened fire? I think they were winching the cage up to let the monster free.'

'Yeah, that makes sense. But that Stefan chap, he's dead,' Fletcher said. 'You kicked his backside last year.'

'You know some of the brothers Oginski shared their knowledge, and their monsters too,' Georgia said. 'But which brother are we dealing with?'

'There are only two left,' Dakkar said. He felt a sting of guilt and sadness. He'd been directly responsible for Kazmer and Stefan Oginski's death in previous adventures, but he was only ever defending himself. Then, towards the end of last year, he'd become involved with a battle between Borys and Tomasz Oginski, a battle that resulted in their deaths and that of his beloved mentor. Franciszek Oginski had taught Dakkar many things, from how to swim in the sea to how to pilot and repair the *Nautilus*. It was Franciszek and Robert Fulton who had invented the *Nautilus* – a smaller version of it, but Dakkar had learned so much when he helped develop the larger version that he had inherited. The submarine had saved Dakkar's life on numerous occasions and, thanks to Tomasz Oginski, it could even fly now with the clever use of hot-air balloons.

'Marek,' Georgia said. 'Tomasz told us he was still alive and active. Blizzard said that Marek had blown up Mount Tambora in the Far East.'

'Why would anyone blow up a volcano?' Fletcher said.

'Blizzard said that the ash thrown up into the sky would cover the sun.' She peered out of the window at the sky. 'He said it would make winter last twelve months. He could be right; it sure doesn't feel like spring. No sun, no crops; no crops, no food. No food; hungry and angry people wanting bread to live.'

'Blimey, that could spark a revolution,' Fletcher murmured. 'Just the kind of trouble Cryptos would take advantage of.'

'It could be the other Oginski brother, Voychek,' Dakkar said. 'But nobody seemed to know much about him or what he even looked like.'

'Surely one of them would know what their own brother looked like!' Fletcher said.

'Apparently, he is a master of disguise.' Georgia shivered. 'When Tomasz talked about him, he seemed really scared.'

Dakkar shrugged and pulled off his wet jacket. 'Well, we need to get these people back to shore so they can go home. We can discuss everything with Commander Blizzard later.'

Georgia turned and pushed the lever by her chair. The *Nautilus* began to surge forward slowly, cutting through the waves and bumping aside beams and cargo that floated on the surface. In the distance, the lights of HMS *Slaughter* winked at them. Dakkar shivered. Fighting Cryptos was always such a thankless job. Cryptos had killed Franciszek Oginski; they caused pain and misery wherever they went. And Dakkar knew he couldn't rest until Cryptos were thwarted. Maybe he wanted revenge for Franciszek Oginski's death. After the last battle with them, Dakkar had said he wouldn't go searching for Cryptos, but when they tried to take slaves, how could he ignore them? He looked out through the window at the huddled crowd in front of the tower. *Even when I rescue people from the chains of slavery*, he thought, *I'm viewed with suspicion. That doesn't mean I shouldn't rescue them, though.*

But what was Cryptos up to? And who was behind this? Dakkar had to find out.

CHAPTER THREE
DANCING

Dressed in dry clothing and sat in Commander Blizzard's cabin on board HMS *Slaughter*, Dakkar felt human once more. He tore the leg off the roast chicken that sat in the centre of the table.

'So, Dakkar, you suspect that one of the Oginski brothers had a hand in this latest slave raid, do you?' Blizzard said, fiddling absent-mindedly with the hook that replaced his hand. He'd lost the lower part of his arm during the battle of Waterloo. One of Stefan Oginski's reptile monsters had bitten it off.

'It has to be. Who else can conjure up monsters like that?' Dakkar said, his mouth full of gravy and chicken.

'Oh really, commander, do we have to put up with such uncouth behaviour?' The young officer opposite Dakkar grimaced at him. 'It's bad enough that we allow his heathen ways on board without inviting him into your cabin!'

Blizzard's face, pale at the best of times, seemed to go paler, making the long scar down his cheek stand out. 'May I remind you, Mr Chudwell, that you may be an earl, but on board my ship you are a mere lieutenant and, as such, will show due respect to *Prince* Dakkar at all times. Do I make myself clear, sir?'

Dakkar glowered over the table at Chudwell, who stared back at him with heavy eyelids. The man was the polar opposite of Blizzard. Where Blizzard had almost unnaturally pale skin, Chudwell was ruddy-faced. His black hair clung to his sweating brow in tight ringlets and he licked his thick lips as he considered what to say next.

'My apologies, commander,' Chudwell said, through gritted teeth. 'I'll remember my . . . place.'

'Be sure that you do,' Blizzard said. 'Prince Dakkar rescued the lives of a whole village today and risked his own life into the bargain.'

An awkward silence fell over the party, interrupted only by the creak of the ship and the clink of cutlery on china.

'Why would Cryptos be taking slaves?' Georgia said at last. 'I mean, it's not as if they don't have manpower for their schemes . . .'

Blizzard popped a cork out of a wine bottle with surprising ease for a man with one hand and poured himself a glass. 'Even Cryptos has to make money from somewhere, I suppose. Their tentacles stretch into all manner of criminal activity.'

'Kidnapping Christian souls from their villages and taking them to Godforsaken lands, for who knows what purpose, seems more than criminal to me, sir,' Chudwell cut in.

'Making *anyone* a slave strikes me as wrong. Christian or not,' Dakkar said, putting his fork down on the table.

'But doesn't your father keep slaves, your *highness*?' Chudwell said, raising his eyebrows.

'It is true that my father, the Rajah of Bundelkhand, has servants, but he doesn't take people from distant lands and make them work for nothing,' Dakkar said. 'That would be barbaric.'

'They didn't bear any of the Cryptos insignia,' Georgia said, seeing an argument on the horizon. Dakkar knew that the Earl of Chudwell's father owned large plantations in the Caribbean. Worked by slaves.

'I have a theory about that,' Blizzard said, taking Georgia's lead. 'I think that often on basic missions Cryptos want to remain unknown. Secrecy is their watchword, after all.'

Dakkar allowed himself to be drawn away from the argument with Chudwell. 'If Cryptos are using Barbary pirates, then that would suggest a base in Africa. Maybe we should investigate.'

'I'm a step ahead of you, Dakkar,' Blizzard said, not catching his eye. 'HMS *Slaughter* sets off for Algiers in the next few days.'

'Excellent!' Dakkar grinned, shaking his fist.

'But you will be staying here,' Blizzard said, raising his eyebrows at Dakkar.

'What?'

'It's a delicate mission, more diplomatic than anything else, but let's just say it doesn't need your ... skills,' Blizzard said. 'Only a week ago, Admiral Lord Exmouth assured us that Algiers would no longer support slave-trading and we've just caught them red-handed ...'

'Except it isn't Algiers, it's Cryptos,' Dakkar said.

'Exactly, but unless I intercept Exmouth, he'll go and bombard the Algerians or something,' Blizzard said. 'It's a bit ticklish ...'

'It requires manners and decorum, eh?' Chudwell grinned slyly across the table. Dakkar felt the blood heat his cheeks. He gritted his teeth.

'But what if something happens?' Dakkar said feebly.

'Things happen all over the world, Dakkar; you can't be everywhere,' Blizzard said briskly, lifting some meat on to his plate with his fork. 'I need you to stay here, with Chudwell ...'

'WHAT?' Dakkar repeated, spraying food across the table.

'He may be a bore ...'

'I say!' Chudwell said.

'But I think he has a point,' Blizzard continued.

'What do you mean?'

'You are an officer in the Royal Navy now, Dakkar, and like it or not, you need to learn some manners.' Blizzard looked hard at Dakkar. 'You've been running around the world, fighting battles and shaking hands with death, for too long. You need to remember how to behave in polite society. Your fellow officers will expect it of you.'

'Hear, hear!' Chudwell said, raising a glass. Blizzard silenced him with a glance.

'Besides, there may be more activity to investigate. I suspect something is afoot. I will let you know what I discover in Algiers when I return.' Blizzard ate a few more mouthfuls, dabbed his face with his handkerchief and stood up. Everyone stood up too, Dakkar included.

'You see,' Blizzard said with a smile. 'You're learning!'

The next few weeks were torment for Dakkar. Blizzard had appointed Chudwell as chief instructor in etiquette and how to behave in society, and Chudwell took to the task with all the enthusiasm of a kitten with its first wounded mouse.

'Don't worry,' Georgia said, sitting with Dakkar at the side of the ballroom. It wasn't late but the chandeliers glowed with candles. Spring seemed a long time coming, the cold was biting and rain lashed the streets of London where Chudwell had brought them.

Dakkar sat with his arms folded, his face set and morose. 'I hate this city,' he said. 'I hate the people in it, the weather, the food. I want to be at sea, on the *Nautilus*.'

He felt trapped in this fancy townhouse with its curtains, log fires and the crush of people; Dakkar felt he could hardly breathe. Every sound grated on him: the braying laughter, the musicians scraping away at fiddles and cellos, even the swish of the huge gowns that the ladies danced in. It all assaulted Dakkar's senses, making him clench his fists until his knuckles whitened.

The quartet playing in the corner of the room struck up a cheerful tune. Georgia jumped up. 'It's a polka. Come and dance with me. I'll show you how.'

Dakkar shrugged her off but she grabbed his elbow and soon he was galloping around the room with Georgia in his arms.

'See?' She laughed. 'It's not so bad . . . Ow! Careful with those feet.'

'Sorry,' Dakkar said, a brief grin flickering across his face.

Dakkar turned around to bow to Georgia and his sword became entangled in another lady's dress. She gave a squeal and he reddened at the sound of tearing fabric as he tried to pull it free.

Blazing with embarrassment, Dakkar gave a short bow and mumbled his apologies. Chuckles and muffled laughter rippled around the room. And Chudwell appeared behind Dakkar.

'Forgive my friend, Lady Elstridge, he is not from these parts, as you can probably tell. Give me a few more weeks with him and I'll have him civilised!'

'What did you say?' Dakkar growled at Chudwell.

'Oh, come on, it was just a joke,' Chudwell said in a low voice. 'Got to have a sense of humour, wot?'

'You'll have me civilised?' Dakkar said, his voice rising. Every eye in the room watched him now.

'Dakkar, calm down. You know what Chudwell's like,' Georgia said, gripping Dakkar's arm.

'And what's that supposed to mean?' Chudwell looked at Georgia as if he'd only just noticed her. 'How would a Yankee backwoods girl like you know anything about conducting oneself?'

This time it was Georgia who reacted. Her arm flicked out so fast that Dakkar hardly saw it. Chudwell's head whipped back and blood spurted from his nose. Women screamed and a number of men rushed forward, not quite sure what to do. Chudwell crumpled to the floor.

'I think we'd better leave,' Dakkar murmured, meeting the hostile gazes of Chudwell's friends.

'Glad to,' Georgia replied. They swept out of the room amid murmurs of shock and mutterings of disapproval.

A carriage took Dakkar and Georgia back to the house. They sat listening to the rattle of the wheels on the cobbles.

'They'll never accept us,' Dakkar said.

'I don't really care if they do or they don't,' Georgia said. 'I'd rather spend my time with the "lower order".'

'You mean ragamuffins like Fletcher?' Dakkar snorted and looked out of the carriage window at the dark streets and the passing houses.

'Now you sound like Chudwell,' Georgia said, her voice flat. They travelled on in silence.

They were staying at a friend of Commander Blizzard's, a retired naval officer called Barrett. He rarely joined them, being old and infirm, but they had the run of the house and servants. Georgia had her own rooms. Unfortunately, they were sharing the house with Chudwell, but he wouldn't be home for many hours, Dakkar thought.

The carriage stopped and they climbed out. A dark figure stood at the gateway to Barrett's imposing town-house. Dakkar narrowed his eyes and tensed, fists raised.

'Who's there?' he said.

A small young man, probably Dakkar's age and dressed in a naval officer's uniform, stepped out of the shadows and extended his hand.

'James Clark-Ross at your service,' he said, grabbing Dakkar's hand and shaking it vigorously. Dakkar stared in surprise at the young man. He had mousey brown hair and quick, sparkling eyes but he looked as if he'd been at sea for some months, judging by his weather-browned skin. 'Commander Blizzard sent me to keep an eye on you. Oh. That sounded a bit odd, didn't it?' He laughed to himself and Dakkar couldn't help smiling too.

'Well, Mr Clark-Ross,' Georgia said, giving a short curtsy. 'We could have done with your assistance a little while ago; the delightful Earl of Chudwell was schooling us in the finer points of ballroom etiquette.'

Clark-Ross's grey-blue eyes clouded over and he frowned. 'Chudwell, yes, dreadful chap. Doesn't know his mizzen mast from his marlin spike.' He clapped his hands. 'A good thing the commander had second thoughts and put me in charge of you both!'

'In charge?' Dakkar said, alarmed.

'Forgive my manners, ma'am. I'm a darned fool at this babysitting game. Put me on a ship and I'm fine but ask me to deal with people on dry land and I'm all at sea. If you see what I mean.' He looked pained. 'Shall we go inside? I'm here to help, honestly.'

CHAPTER FOUR
MURDERER!

James Clark-Ross proved to be excellent company. They sat by the fire eating toast and listening to his stories.

'My uncle is Sir John Ross,' James said through a mouthful of crumbs. 'He's a commander, like Blizzard but without the hook for a hand and the icy stare.'

'We've sailed with Blizzard many a time,' Georgia said. James's eyes widened.

'You have? You too, Miss Georgia?'

'Even though I'm a mere slip of a girl, yes,' Georgia said, smiling. It was hard to be annoyed by Clark-Ross. 'I've fought alongside him.'

'Georgia is a better shot than me,' Dakkar said, smiling at James's slack-jawed stare.

'Do forgive me, Miss Georgia, but that is capital!' He slapped his hand down on his knee. Then he sighed. 'I could do with a good battle. We patrol the Channel, hoping for some action, but nothing ever happens these days.'

'I should think everyone will be glad of the peace since Waterloo,' Dakkar said, but he knew what James meant. Even though his last encounter with the pirates was only weeks ago, he longed to be on the sea with a sense of purpose again.

'Not everyone,' James said with a sigh. 'Many of our soldiers are returning from the continent only to find there is little work. These are dangerous times . . .'

'Dangerous?' Georgia said, frowning. 'Why?'

James lowered his voice and glanced around as if someone might be hiding behind the curtains, listening. 'Some say that the King is sick. That he has gone mad. He is kept in his palace, away from public view. His son tries to take on the job of ruling but he is more interested in music and, if you'll pardon me, miss, women!'

'So you think there is a danger that soldiers coming back from the wars will rebel against the King?' Dakkar gasped.

'France wasn't the first country in Europe to chop its ruler's head off,' James said ominously. 'England was. The government is terrified of revolution here.'

'It makes you wonder,' Dakkar said, thinking aloud, 'what use Cryptos would make of such discontent.'

'You think they might be round here, stirring up trouble?' Georgia said, the firelight reflected in her wide eyes.

'It's possible,' Dakkar murmured.

'Here's a bit of a mystery too.' James waggled his

eyebrows and leaned forward. 'A ship has just docked in the last few days from Algiers.'

'Really?' Dakkar sat up. 'But we encountered some Barbary pirates only a few weeks ago. Is it a legal vessel?'

Clark-Ross nodded. 'But how often do you see a Barbary ship on the Thames? She's called the *Serqet*.'

'That's a strange name,' Georgia said. 'Is it foreign? What does it mean?'

Clark-Ross shrugged. 'Damned if I know.' He grinned. 'But it's a strange kettle of fish. I've a mind to go and have a look at her.'

'The *Serqet*,' Dakkar said. 'It's familiar but I can't place it. I've heard it before, maybe in my studies with Oginski . . .'

At that moment the front door crashed open. Dakkar could hear Chudwell's slurred, drunken voice in the hall.

'Out of my way, man; take my coat, here!' he bellowed at the manservant who had come to help him.

Now Chudwell stood at the door to the drawing room and stared in at Dakkar, Georgia and James. He swayed and gripped the door frame.

'You disgraced me, sir,' he said, pointing a shaking finger at Dakkar. 'I will have satisfaction . . .'

'Just name the time, you drunken fop!' Dakkar snarled, leaping to his feet. Georgia grabbed his arm, holding him back.

'Gentlemen, gentlemen,' James said in a soothing voice. He jumped up and took Chudwell by the shoulder.

'What's done is done, eh? You look worn out. Let me help you to your room.'

Chudwell tried to shake James off but James proved stronger than he looked. Soon all Dakkar could hear was Chudwell's muffled complaints as James led him up the stairs. Georgia looked archly at Dakkar.

'Well, that will come back to bother us in the morning, I'm certain,' she said.

'I wasn't the one who punched him,' Dakkar pointed out. He sighed. 'But if he wants trouble, he's come to the right person.'

'Easy, Dakkar,' Georgia said, still holding his hand. 'Forget Chudwell. He's not worth bothering with.'

'I'm telling you, I'm just in the mood to settle a few scores,' Dakkar said moodily.

Dakkar slept badly. His encounter with Chudwell kept flashing into his mind, as did the images of the wary prisoners he'd helped to rescue from the pirates. *And what were those pirates up to? Was it just a slave run, capturing people for profit? Or was there an Oginski out there, lurking and waiting to strike?*

He sat up and rubbed his face. Darkness still filled the room and he had no idea of the time.

A thud and a muffled cry came from next door. Dakkar leapt out of bed. It hadn't sounded like someone stumbling in the night. That was a cry of terror and pain.

Rushing out on to the landing of the grand house,

Dakkar scanned around in the feeble glow of the trimmed oil lamps that stood on the table by his room.

Chudwell's door stood open and a strange strangled cry came from the room beyond. Without thinking, Dakkar snatched up the oil lamp and dashed into the room. He stopped with a gasp.

Chudwell lay on the bed with a dagger sticking from his chest. His eyes stared wide at Dakkar and his face had a bluish tinge suggesting poison. Dakkar inched forward, checking behind the door for any possible assailants. Then he ran and snatched the dagger from Chudwell's body. It was too late: the man was dead.

Dakkar ran across to the open window and saw a dark, turbaned figure disappearing over the wall of the house.

'What's going on here?' James appeared with several manservants armed with guns. Dakkar looked back, knife still in his hand and his leg halfway across the windowsill as he prepared to give chase to the killer. 'I say, what have you done?'

'James. What do you mean?' Dakkar looked down. Blood from the dagger had splashed on to his nightshirt. Realisation dawned on him. 'James, it wasn't me. There was a man. He ran into the street. I was about to chase him . . .'

'Shall I call the constable, Mr Clark-Ross?' one of the manservants said, levelling a shotgun at Dakkar.

'I think you had better,' James said, staring at Chudwell's body.

'It's not what you think!' Dakkar insisted, taking a step forward. The manservant raised the gun a little and Dakkar froze. He glanced around the room for some means of escape but he was too close to the gun. One move and he'd be blown apart.

'Dakkar, you're holding a knife, you have Chudwell's blood on your clothes and I come in to find you climbing out of the window,' James said. 'What am I meant to think?'

Georgia burst in. 'Dakkar, what's . . . ?' Her question died as her eyes flicked from Chudwell to Dakkar. 'Dakkar, did you . . . ?'

'NO!' Dakkar yelled. 'I heard a noise and found Chudwell dead. I took the dagger from his body. Look at the handle. I don't own a knife like this.' He held the knife out for someone to take. 'Be careful, I think the blade may be poisoned.'

James took it from him between thumb and forefinger, grimacing at the blood. The handle had a scorpion engraved on it.

'That's true,' Georgia said, frowning at the dagger. 'I've never seen a weapon like that.'

'Well, you would say that, wouldn't you,' James said, pulling out a handkerchief and wiping the dagger clean. 'I'd do the same for a friend of mine. The fact remains that I saw Dakkar trying to climb out of the window, as did these men here. The constable will be along in a minute. I suggest you don't try to escape.'

'Are you saying I'm lying?' Georgia said, her cheeks reddening.

'I'd never call a lady a liar,' James said, with a sad smile. 'But we have to let the constable decide or there'll be even worse scandal and possibly a lynch mob of lords and ladies after Dakkar.'

'But I didn't do it!'

'That may be true, your highness,' James said. 'But we have to follow the rule of law, and I'll be honest: things don't look good for you.'

CHAPTER FIVE
PRISONER

The prison cell stank of filth and stale bodies. Dakkar sat on a straw pallet staring at the chains on the floor. He'd unlocked the manacles around his wrists and ankles in a matter of minutes using his belt buckle. Franciszek Oginski had taught him everything he knew about all things mechanical, including locks. Now he wondered how effective a weapon the chains would make.

The dank cell heaved with bodies. Men huddled in every corner, watching each other, watching him. They were crushed against one another, shoving each other and trying to make some room. The cold seeped from every damp stone of this dingy place. A thin, grey light filtered in from a tiny window set high in the wall, almost at ceiling level.

A skinny, rat-faced old man sidled over to Dakkar and ran a finger down the fabric of his jacket.

'What's a fine young gent like you doing in a place like

this then, eh?' The man cackled and a few others nearby joined in. Dakkar clenched his teeth.

'I'm accused of murder,' he said, staring coldly at the man.

Dakkar had gone quietly with the constable, not wanting to make himself look even guiltier, but now the prospects seemed bleak. He could see how his guilt became more and more confirmed with each retelling. It was like a game he used to play when he was a small child. You whispered a phrase into your friend's ear and they passed it on, and by the time it reached the last hearer, the meaning of the message had completely changed. Dakkar had seen this happen already.

'I found his highness holding the dagger and trying to climb out of the window,' James Clark-Ross had said. 'He's says he was after a third party, though. So, erm, he mightn't have done it, if you see what I mean.'

The constable had insisted on taking Dakkar to prison despite Dakkar and Georgia's protestations. When he'd got Dakkar there, he'd said to the guard, 'Watch this one, caught red-handed, literally. Blood everywhere, knife in his hand. He gutted the Earl of Chudwell.'

By the time this comes to a trial, they'll have convinced themselves I'm guilty, Dakkar thought, weighing his manacles in his hands. *I can't wait for that.*

'And did ye?' said Rat-face, snapping him back to the present.

'Of course not,' Dakkar said.

Rat-face looked slyly at two other men who had joined

them. 'No, we're all innocent in 'ere, aren't we, lads,' he chuckled. 'Never done nuffin' wrong! But don't worry, your lordship, we'll take care of yer.' The men joined in with his laughter.

Dakkar grabbed Rat-face's wrist and stood up, wrenching the man's arm up behind his back. 'I can take care of myself,' Dakkar hissed, throwing the man into his two accomplices.

Rat-face picked himself up, massaging his arm. 'All right, no need to get so shirty,' he muttered. But Dakkar had made his point and a space cleared around him as men shuffled back.

Dakkar peered through the grille in the thick wooden door. One guard sat eating at a table. Another thick wooden door stood behind him. Just how big was the prison? It had looked imposing and dark when Dakkar had been brought here. He'd counted three doors and had a rough idea of how many lefts and rights would get him to the front, but how many guards were there along the way?

Time crawled past. Dakkar tried to ignore the smell and misery around him. He looked at the men squatting and lying in a sordid heap around him. *Their main crime is being poor*, he thought. *Soldiers come back from fighting in France and finding no welcome and no work.*

Finally a guard appeared at the grille and called his name. Dakkar jumped up and came to the door, fixing his manacles loosely around his ankles so that the guard didn't notice he'd unlocked them.

Georgia and Fletcher stood at the open door, pale and worried.

'We tried to get a message to Blizzard but he's too far away,' Georgia said, her voice shaking.

'If you did do it, then I reckon Chudwell had it coming,' Fletcher said angrily.

'I didn't do it!' Dakkar hissed, slamming his fists on the door frame.

'You were provoked, Dakkar, I saw that,' Georgia began.

'You think I did it, don't you?'

Georgia dropped her eyes to the floor 'No, no! But you were standing there with the knife and –' She stopped but then decided to carry on. 'And that temper of yours can get out of control sometimes. I don't know what to think.'

Dakkar turned away from her. 'I thought you of all people would know I didn't do it.'

'But you're so hot-headed sometimes, Dakkar.' Georgia grabbed Dakkar's arm. 'Sometimes you do something first and think about it later . . .'

'I'm not a murderer,' Dakkar said, shaking her off. 'You should know that.'

Georgia looked drawn and worried. 'Chudwell's family are crying out for blood and they have connections,' she said. 'Rumour has it that Chudwell's uncle, Justice Parbright, is pressing to hear the trial tomorrow.'

'Tomorrow?' Dakkar gasped. 'So soon?'

'At noon! If they find you guilty, they'll take you

out and hang you on the spot,' Fletcher said, his voice hoarse.

'You have to break me out of here,' Dakkar said. 'Get the *Nautilus* ready. We've got to escape.'

'But how?' Fletcher said, glancing round at the guards, who seemed not to be paying attention. 'Look, this place is like a fortress.'

'We've got out of tighter scrapes than this.' Dakkar grinned. 'Haven't we, Georgia?'

'But you'll be a fugitive,' Georgia said, looking worried. 'You've got to clear your name!'

'And is that likely to happen when they are going to hang me tomorrow?' Dakkar said darkly. 'No, you go. It looks like I'm on my own.' He turned to walk back into the cell.

'Dakkar, wait!' Georgia grabbed his arm and looked him in the eyes. 'We're your friends. We believe in you. We'll get you out. Right, Fletcher?'

'I can't believe we're going to do this,' Fletcher said, putting his hands to his head. Then he broke into a grin. 'Yeah, you can count on us.'

Dakkar smiled. Georgia and Fletcher were true friends. 'I'll need some of my clockwork toys,' he said, his voice barely a whisper. 'And pistols. Find out as much as you can about the layout of the courtroom too.'

'Do you have a plan?' Georgia said.

Dakkar shrugged. 'I think we create a distraction and then make it up as we go along,' he said.

Fletcher slapped him on the shoulder. 'Don't worry, Dax, me old mate,' he said. 'This time tomorrow you'll be free as a bird.'

'Or dead as a doornail,' Dakkar added grimly.

Georgia smiled. 'Nothing new there then,' she said.

CHAPTER SIX
TRIAL

The courtroom smelt almost as bad as the cell that Dakkar had just been brought up from. It was more crowded too. People had heard of the strange Indian prince who had murdered an earl and crowds had piled into the room to catch a glimpse of him. It was a proper spectator event. Dakkar could even hear women hawking bags of nuts outside. Dakkar's stomach rumbled. It was midday and he'd spent all morning in the foul prison. Thinking he'd need his strength for his escape, he'd managed to force down the thin gruel they'd served him.

Eager observers crammed the galleries and balcony above, chattering excitedly and pointing as Dakkar was led in, his manacles still loosely fastened.

The room reminded Dakkar of a chapel; dark wooden panels lined the walls and people sat on long pews. At one end the wall was completely filled by a wooden box and in that sat the judge on a large throne. Justice Parbright glared out at Dakkar as he was led up to another box reserved for the accused.

'Is this the fellow who murdered my nephew?' he said, pointing a long bony finger at Dakkar. Parbright filled the throne, a tall man but old and skeletal. His long white wig made his face look even longer.

Dakkar scanned the sea of faces for Georgia and Fletcher but couldn't see them. James Clark-Ross stood in his best naval uniform.

'It is the accused, your honour,' a clerk said, nervously bowing.

'May I speak, your honour?' James called out.

Justice Parbright curled a lip at James. 'Much good it'll do him,' the judge said. 'Come on, say your piece, man. I'm hungry and I haven't had my luncheon yet. I want to get this over with!'

'Sir, I don't think Prince Dakkar is guilty of the earl's murder,' James said. 'He is a young man of good character and would be vouched for by Commander Blizzard . . .'

'Bring Blizzard in then, why don't you?' Parbright said, waving his gavel at the door as if Blizzard could be called.

James looked nonplussed. 'Well, I can't; I mean, no. The commander is away on the King's business at the moment and cannot be contacted . . .'

'Then there's no point in bringing his name up, lad,' Parbright snarled. 'You were there that night?'

'Yes, sir,' James said, his neck and cheeks colouring.

'And tell me what you saw,' Parbright said, an unpleasant smile spreading across his face.

'Well, I . . . saw . . . Prince Dakkar holding a knife,' James said, breaking eye contact with Parbright. The crowd murmured excitedly.

'And where was this?'

'Why, in Sir Chudwell's room, but . . .'

'And what was Prince Dakkar doing when you entered the room?'

James looked defeated, his shoulders slumped. 'He was about to climb out of the window.'

The crowd burst into a roar of discussion that had Parbright smacking his gavel down on the plate so hard it looked as if it would break.

Dakkar continued to search for Georgia or Fletcher. *Perhaps they hadn't been able to squeeze in*, he thought.

'So, you find Prince Dakkar soaked in my nephew's blood, holding a dagger and trying to climb out of his bedroom window, and you think he might not be guilty? A mere boy, barely out of school, presumes to come here and tell me my job?'

'But, with respect, sir –' James began.

Dakkar desperately scanned the crowd and locked eyes on Georgia at last. She gave a tight smile and a nod.

'Respect, sir? Respect!' Parbright slammed his gavel down and this time the head flew off. 'If you had more respect, you wouldn't have shown your gormless face in here this morning! No, sir. He's guilty! As plain as the nose on your face. Guilty!' He turned his grey face to

Dakkar. 'Have you anything to say before they take you out and hang you?'

'Yes, your honour,' Dakkar said. He glanced over to Georgia and let his manacles slip free. 'I am innocent!' he bellowed, as a gunshot went off, followed by a muffled explosion. Choking black smoke spewed across the crowd at the back of the room and they stampeded towards the judge's chair, turning tables and pews over and sending a storm of papers into the air.

Dakkar glimpsed two clockwork dogs waddling across the floor. He recognised his own handiwork. These were one of Dakkar's inventions: stun grenades that walked towards their targets, designed to confuse rather than kill. He gave a fleeting grin just before they went off with a bang. More smoke filled the room. And the crowd pushed away from it, knocking guards and clerks to the floor.

Georgia and Fletcher appeared at Dakkar's side.

'This way,' Georgia panted, grabbing Dakkar's arm.

'Stop them!' Parbright roared, but the smoke and crowd made hearing or seeing anything too difficult. Another gunshot went off and a foul smell filled the room that made Dakkar's eyes water. Women screamed and guards shouted useless commands as more furniture went crashing down and people blundered about in the fog of smoke.

'Go for that door to the side of Parbright's chair,' Georgia said, pushing Dakkar towards it. He saw Parbright dimly through the smoke, coughing and rubbing his eyes. He paused and stared at Dakkar.

'They're here! Over here!' Parbright yelled, coughing between every word, but the smoke had taken the strength from his voice.

Suddenly they were going through a panelled door and into a resting chamber behind the courtroom where judges made their deliberations and changed their robes.

Fletcher grabbed an apple that lay in a fruit bowl on a small table. 'This way,' he said, crunching into the apple and heading for a door at the other side of the room.

This door swung open and a maid carrying a tray of glasses and a decanter of brandy stepped into the room, her eyes widening. Dakkar, Georgia and Fletcher almost ran into her and she fainted, dropping the tray with a crash.

'What a waste.' Fletcher grinned, looking back at the puddle of brandy as Georgia led them through a maze of passages.

'The servants use these to get to the judge's room without disturbing people in other rooms,' she explained.

'She's been sweet-talking one of the clerks,' Fletcher said as they ran. 'Told her all about the place. Even drew her a map!'

'This should be the kitchen,' Georgia said, pushing open another heavy wooden door.

They burst into the kitchen, where a number of servants screamed and dropped pots and plates. The smell of roast chicken made Dakkar's mouth water and he glimpsed Fletcher snatching up a whole carcass and taking a huge bite out of it.

'Got to eat when you can,' Fletcher said, sounding almost apologetic.

Georgia pushed the kitchen door open and they stumbled out into the smoky streets. Dakkar drew a breath, savouring his freedom. They stood in a narrow side alley that separated the courthouse from the shops and houses around it.

'Don't look now, but I think they're on to us,' Dakkar said at the sound of heavy boots rattling on the cobbles.

'This way!' Fletcher snapped, leading them away from the approaching guards. A bullet whined past them and Dakkar glanced back to see red coats and flashing blades.

'Soldiers!' Georgia shouted.

'Left!' Fletcher yelled, and seemed to vanish into a solid brick wall. Dakkar followed him and saw another narrow alley, barely wide enough to walk up. The shadows closed in on them. It was mid-afternoon but the clouds above blotted out the sun and the tall buildings on either side of the alley did the rest.

The passage widened but they hadn't lost their pursuers yet. Another bullet buzzed over Dakkar's head and one cracked the brickwork close to Georgia. The passages and alleys twisted and turned, widening and narrowing. Dakkar stumbled past intersections and through court-yards. Their feet splashed in puddles of stagnant water. People yelled as they barged past them. *So many people*, Dakkar thought. *I wish I was back on the sea. Or better, under it!*

'Here,' Fletcher yelled. They ran on, pounding through the narrow back streets between ramshackle buildings that leaned in as if they might collapse at any minute. It grew darker, if that were possible, and the smell from the filth on the cobbles and from the houses all around them grew worse. Dakkar glanced back as they crossed another shadowy courtyard.

'They're still following,' Georgia moaned.

'No, look!' Dakkar hissed, slowing down. The soldiers faltered, looking at each other, uncertain what to do.

'We're entering the Holy Land.' Fletcher grinned. 'They're wary of following!'

Dakkar frowned. 'The Holy Land?'

'St Giles! The roughest, meanest pigsty in London,' Fletcher said proudly. 'Nobody's safe here. Not even the army.'

'And not us,' Georgia said.

'I am,' Fletcher said. 'I grew up round here.'

'We might need your local connections then,' Dakkar said, as three scruffy, dirt-covered men peeled themselves from the shadows and crept towards them.

CHAPTER SEVEN
FLASH COMPANY

Dakkar weighed up their chances as the three men sauntered across the courtyard. They weren't the healthiest specimens, skinny and unwashed, their lank hair hanging down to their shoulders under holey woollen hats. One of them had a limp and their skin looked grey and lifeless. *They won't pose much of a problem*, Dakkar thought. *But we're on their home ground. How many friends have they got? Where can we run?*

'Is that you, Fletcher?' the nearest scruff said as he approached them. 'What you doin' back 'ere? I thought you took the King's shillin'.'

'Reegan Scribbly, as I live an' breathe,' Fletcher said, as if he'd just found a long-lost brother. 'How're you keepin'?'

Reegan sniffed and scratched a stubbly chin. 'Hard times, Jim. Hard times.' He looked Dakkar up and down. 'Who's this? Not from round 'ere, that's a fact.'

Fletcher sidled closer to Reegan and brought his head close. 'It's a bit delicate: we're being chased by the King's men.'

Reegan's eyes narrowed but Dakkar noticed he stooped a little less; his cheeks reddened too. 'There's no love lost between us and the peelers, or the King's men, right, lads?' Reegan turned to his two ragged accomplices, who both nodded in agreement. He leaned a bit closer to Fletcher. 'In fact,' Scribbly said, tapping the side of his nose, 'there's revolution in the air. If you fancy some easy money, causin' a bit of trouble, call in at Ma Crampley's. I can put you in touch wiv the right people.'

'Interestin',' Fletcher said. 'Ma Crampley's it is then, for a glass and a bit of a chinwag?'

Reegan tapped the side of his nose. 'If anyone asks me, I ain't seen yer!'

Fletcher led the way through the twisting alleys and Georgia and Dakkar followed. The stink of filth thrown into the street made Dakkar choke. Dead things, dogs and other carcasses, lay in the clogged gutters. All around him people argued and jostled; a few stopped to stare at them. Some people nodded to Fletcher.

'You seem to be well known in these parts,' Georgia said to Fletcher as they hurried along.

'Lived here for a while after me old dad died,' Fletcher said. 'Did a few jobs for a lot of people.'

'Jobs? You mean thieving?' Dakkar said.

'Did what I could to survive.' Fletcher grinned. He looked closely at Dakkar. 'Not your kind of place then?'

'It's too crowded,' Dakkar said. 'I prefer the sea.'

'Well, you couldn't get much further from that, Dakkar!' Fletcher chuckled. 'This is the most crowded and Godforsaken hole in the country.'

'You can say that again,' Georgia muttered, stepping over a dead cat.

'But you won't get trouble from the law,' Fletcher said, winking at Dakkar. 'At least, not for a while. There's a few constables who patrol this place but we can buy them off.'

Ma Crampley's was a crumbling ruin of a building on the corner of two alleyways so narrow that Dakkar wondered how anyone got down them. Inside wasn't much better than out. The rotten door opened into a large room with a bar at the back and a stairway leading to a balcony that overlooked the room.

Dakkar wrinkled his nose at the smell of cheap candles, tobacco and unwashed bodies. The place was heaving with people, and sounds of laughter, screams and shouting mingled with music from a blind fiddler who scraped away in the corner. People huddled around tables, drinking and squinting at playing cards in the dim candlelight.

'Come on.' Fletcher led them across the room to an empty table. An old lady dressed in ragged silks appeared at their side. Powder and make-up caked her face and old, sad-looking feathers drooped from her wig.

'So, Fletcher, you came back to see old Ma Crampley

then?' The woman gave a black-toothed grin and pinched his cheek. 'How's me favourite young man?'

'Hello, Ma.' Fletcher grinned and gave the old woman a hug. Ma Crampley stared at Dakkar over his shoulder.

'And who do we have here?' she said, her eyes roving over Dakkar, sizing him up and measuring him. Her grin broadened. 'I heard tell of a kerfuffle at the courtrooms not long ago. That weren't you, was it?'

'Ma,' Fletcher said reproachfully. 'What do you take us for? Common criminals?'

Ma Crampley cackled and gave Fletcher's shoulder a feeble smack. 'We're all common criminals 'ere, Fletch! So, what's the story?'

'Get us some refreshment and I'll let you in on the secret!' Fletcher said, winking. 'But I'll want all the gossip in return, mind!'

The old woman bustled off, pushing a few drunken punters aside in her hurry. Fletcher sat down and leaned towards Dakkar and Georgia. 'Now listen closely,' he said. 'Ma Crampley's a wily old bird. Don't be fooled by her dotty appearance. She's as sly as a fox and twice as quick. She hates the peelers but loves hard cash. Let me do all the talking.'

Dakkar nodded.

Ma Crampley came back with a bottle and grimy glasses on a tray. 'Here,' she said, setting the tray down. She settled on to another chair and grinned again. 'Now, what's goin' on?'

'Lieutenant Baudin,' Fletcher said in a low voice,

pointing to Dakkar, 'and Miss Nugent' – he pointed to Georgia – 'have eloped.'

'What???' Dakkar spluttered. He felt his face reddening. Georgia's face split into an amused grin.

'It's fine, monsieur,' Ma Crampley said, laying a hand on Dakkar's arm. 'Your secret is safe with me!' She pulled a grubby handkerchief from her sleeve and blew her nose. 'I was young once. What is it? Her father doesn't approve?'

'He's a brute,' Georgia said, clearly enjoying Dakkar's discomfort and trying not to laugh. 'He wouldn't even let poor old Henri, here, into the house. But tonight we're going up to Scotland to be married!' She clung on to Dakkar's arm a little too tightly.

'Yes,' Dakkar said through gritted teeth and glaring at Fletcher. 'I can't wait!'

Ma Crampley stood up, dabbing her eyes. 'Well, I wish you all the luck, my dears. Your secret is safe with me!'

Fletcher grabbed Ma Crampley's arm to stop her walking away. 'Don't rush off, Ma,' he said, grinning. 'There must be lots of gossip to share!'

The old woman sat down slowly and poured herself a drink. 'Well,' she said, glancing around. 'Old Bill Tanner has been up to his tricks again, flogging stolen horses, but' – she leaned so close to Fletcher and Dakkar that he had to hold his breath – 'rumours are growin'. Someone's up to no good. Buildin' an army.'

'An army?' Dakkar repeated. Ma Crampley slapped her scrawny hand around Dakkar's wrist, making him jump.

'Not so loud,' she said. 'An army. I've heard murderous and rebellious talk in this house. People say they've no jobs, no money. They say they're starvin' but they still come in here and buy gin. They blame the King, say he's mad . . .'

'Who does, Ma?' Fletcher said.

'Everyone,' she said. 'There's a lot of people here come back from fighting the French and found they've got nothing. Strangers have been offering good wages, food and shelter to veterans who'll join them.'

'That Scribbly fella mentioned something along those lines,' Georgia said.

'Strangers,' Dakkar said. 'Are there any in here now?'

'Him over there.' Ma nodded to a man leaning against the bar. 'I've overheard him tryin' to get some soldiers to join him. He's a sailor from an Algerian ship – the *Serqet*, it's called, or something. He's proper trouble and no mistake . . .'

'The *Serqet*? That's the second time we've heard the name of that ship,' Georgia said to Dakkar.

But Dakkar didn't answer. His eyes were locked on the man at the bar.

He was tall and burly, weathered by many years at sea. A grubby turban covered most of his straggly grey hair. His blue jacket suggested a stint in His Majesty's Navy but his baggy trousers reminded Dakkar of the pirates he'd met off the coast of Cornwall. But it was the knife poking out of his belt that really drew Dakkar's attention. A knife with a scorpion handle.

The man looked around and caught Dakkar's eye for a split second. It was enough. He mumbled something under his breath and sprang from the bar, barging people out of the way as he sprinted for the door.

CHAPTER EIGHT
DEATH CHASE

Sending his chair clattering, Dakkar threw himself towards the fleeing man. A woman screamed and someone yelled a curse as the man pushed them out of the way.

'He's the man who killed Chudwell!' Dakkar shouted at the others, who still sat bewildered.

Evening was falling and shadows filled the murky alleyway that Dakkar stumbled out into. The sound of yells and heavy footsteps told him straight away which direction the man had gone.

'Dakkar, wait!' Georgia called from behind him, but Dakkar hurried after the man.

'If we can catch him, we can prove my innocence!' Dakkar called back, and then barged through a line of drunken women staggering down the passage.

The man was fast but Dakkar was younger and quicker. Dakkar dodged between gangs of people where the man crashed into them. He leapt over the barrels and boxes that the man overturned in his path.

They ducked and dived, twisting right and left, until Dakkar had no idea where he was or how to get back to Ma Crampley's. The darkness grew into a total blackness. There were no lamps here and the high buildings blotted out any moonlight from the filthy, cramped alleys. Dakkar slowed down. Here and there a shout rang out, but otherwise he could only hear his panting breath.

Where is he? Dakkar thought.

Something whizzed past his ear and buried itself in the wooden door frame close to him. Dakkar glimpsed the scorpion-handled knife vibrating with the force of the throw. Then a heavy body struck him, sending him sprawling to the floor like a ragdoll. Dakkar gasped for breath as a fist smacked into his ribs.

Regaining his senses, Dakkar swung his head forward and saw stars as he connected with his attacker's chin. It worked, though. The man was disorientated and rolled off Dakkar. Not pausing, Dakkar struck out blindly with his fist and cracked into the side of the man's head.

The man grunted but he was obviously tough and used to close combat. He closed his fingers around Dakkar's throat. Dakkar punched and kicked at the man's stomach and ribs, making him grunt with pain, but he didn't let go. In desperation, Dakkar gripped the man's hands, focusing on his thumbs, and began to crush them against his palms. Dakkar's vision was failing and his head pounded but he squeezed harder. The man's grip weakened and Dakkar continued to squeeze the man's thumbs, making him yell and pull back. But Dakkar felt weak. He gasped for breath as the alley swirled around him.

'Dakkar!' Fletcher's voice rang out across the alley.

Dakkar heard the metallic click of a pistol hammer being pulled back. 'Don't move, mister.' Georgia's voice was full of menace. Dakkar felt the man freeze for a second.

Slowly, the world came back into focus and Dakkar saw his two friends standing over them. Georgia had a pistol pointed at the man.

'Are you all right, Dakkar?' Fletcher said, dragging him to his feet. Dakkar nodded but the world still swam around him.

'Start talkin', mister,' Georgia said, twitching the pistol.

'Never!' the man snarled and whipped something from his pocket. He stuffed it into his mouth before Georgia could react. The sailor's eyes widened and his lips turned blue. Then his face twisted and he fell to the floor, writhing in agony.

Fletcher rushed forward and turned the twitching man over. 'Poison,' he said.

'Very fast-acting poison,' Dakkar said, his voice hoarse. He stumbled forward. 'And look.' The man's jacket had fallen open, revealing his bare chest and a tattoo of a scorpion, pincers open and tail curling around his side. 'The men on the pirate ship had that tattoo,' Dakkar said, frowning.

'And that dagger you found in Chudwell's room had a

scorpion on the handle,' Georgia added. 'Do you think this man was the killer?'

'I thought so at first, but look.' Dakkar pulled the dagger that had been thrown at him from the woodwork. 'This knife is identical. Unless the killer had two knives the same, I don't think this is our man, but he recognised me. That's why he ran.'

'There must be some kind of link,' Fletcher said, squinting at the knife. 'Y'don't see many blades like that round 'ere. An' this feller was recruiting men who had come back from the wars . . .'

'And he had the same tattoo as the pirates on that Cryptos ship,' Dakkar said. 'Which suggests that Cryptos are planning something big. Here.'

'You think they're building an army?' Georgia said, looking alarmed. 'Right here in the capital?'

'It certainly sounds like it and Ma Crampley said this man came from the *Serqet*,' Dakkar said. 'Scorpions. That's the link.'

Georgia looked puzzled. 'What do you mean?'

'The *Serqet*,' Dakkar said faintly. 'I've remembered what that means now. Serqet was an Ancient Egyptian goddess. She took the form of a scorpion . . .'

Fletcher rubbed his chin. 'And we have a killer with a scorpion-handled knife, a man with the same knife and a scorpion tattoo like the pirates',' he said.

'Put like that,' Georgia said, 'there's got to be a link! I reckon it must be Cryptos, judging by the monster you fought on the pirate ship.'

'We should move along as quick as we can,' Fletcher said, glancing nervously around. 'Folk will be watchin'. We need to get away before someone blames you for this murder too, Dakkar!'

'We'll head down to the docks and see if we can't get a look at the ship,' Dakkar said. 'If we get down there, maybe we'll find evidence that will clear my name.'

Fletcher grinned. 'Follow me,' he said.

They hurried through the twisting maze of cramped alleys. Dakkar marvelled at how well Fletcher knew his way around.

'When you're bein' chased by the peelers, you have to know all the short cuts and all the nooks!' he shouted as they splashed through muddy courtyards and rubbish-choked passages. Once or twice, they actually scurried through people's houses.

Dakkar screwed his face up at the stink and filth. 'Why do people live like this?' he said.

'Don't have much choice,' Fletcher said, panting as they ran. 'When you're poor and out of work, you live as best you can. Some of these rooms have three or four families in them. It's no wonder if someone is stirring up trouble here.'

'Horrible,' Dakkar said. He couldn't help thinking of the rich ballroom he'd been in only the other night and all the people there dancing as if they didn't have a care in the world.

The slums thinned out and they stumbled on to a wider street where carriages rattled up and down. Fletcher pressed himself against the wall of the great building they stood by.

'Keep to the shadows here,' he said. 'Remember, you're wanted for murder. That mightn't count for much in the slums we've just come from, but out here you're fair game and the peelers'll have you if you're spotted.'

The stink of the river grew as they neared it, but Dakkar found the cry of sailors and the ring of bells reassuring. He was nearer the sea.

A tangle of wooden piers poked out into the river. Some ships were moored in the middle of the water and could only be accessed by rowing boat. The water was high and the moon's reflection wobbled clear and fat on the surface.

'Which one is it?' Georgia whispered as they neared the edge of the river. It was hard to distinguish one ship from another in the forest of masts that rocked on the water. Ropes and furled sails hung from beams like vines and creepers in a jungle.

'That one?' Dakkar pointed to a ship, slightly apart from the others and lashed to the end of a long pier. It looked much smaller than many of the craft there and more weathered.

They crept to the pier and hid behind a pile of crates that stood there. 'What's the plan?' Fletcher whispered.

'I don't know,' Dakkar said. 'If we can get closer, we'll be able to see if any of the crew have scorpion tattoos. Maybe we can persuade James Clarke-Ross to bring some men down to question the captain and the crew . . .'

'Sounds a bit sketchy,' Fletcher said, pulling a face. Then he grinned. 'I like it.'

Dakkar shrugged. 'If we can find some kind of evidence. Maybe other crewmen will have scorpion daggers. That would suggest that someone on board was at least involved in Chudwell's murder.'

Georgia nodded. 'Fair enough,' she said and peered over the crates. 'But you're going to have to be fast!'

A shout went up on the ship and Dakkar heard the sound of feet on the deck. He joined Georgia. Men were scurrying all over the deck and climbing up the mast to unfurl the sails.

'They're getting ready to set sail,' he gasped.

Keeping low, they scampered further along the pier, crouching behind some empty barrels.

'Can you see anything?' Georgia hissed.

'No,' Dakkar murmured. 'We're going to have to get closer. If we could capture one of the men, then we could take him back for questioning.'

Some crew members were actually on the pier, loading a few last supplies. A large crate swung above them as it was winched on to the ship. Dakkar could see one smaller sailor leaning against some bales.

'Maybe we could overpower him without being spotted,' Dakkar said.

'It's risky,' Fletcher said. His face looked pale in the moonlight.

'If we don't do something soon, they'll be gone,' Georgia said. 'The dead man back in the slums won't be answering any questions.'

'His body'll be long gone,' Fletcher said, giving a humourless grin. 'Let's do it.'

Dakkar slipped from behind the barrels and scurried across to the bales. In one fluid movement, he closed his hand across the man's face and pulled him back. Georgia rapped him on the temple with the handle of her pistol and the sailor crumpled to the ground.

Something flickered in the half-light and, at first, Dakkar thought it was a snake. He leapt back and then gasped. It was a rope.

The sailor had been holding one of the ropes that held the crate in the air. Now the line whipped and flicked upward as the crate jerked sideways. The sudden extra weight took the men on the boat who also held the rope by surprise. They released their hold and the crate came crashing to the ground.

'Quickly, help me carry him,' Dakkar snapped.

But Fletcher and Georgia stood frozen and staring at where the crate had landed. Dakkar looked too and swallowed hard.

The planks of the crate lay in a crazy jumble but something black and shining had wriggled its way out of the mess of wood. Now it rolled open and began to move on hundreds of undulating legs. Dakkar had seen millipedes in his homeland but this one was the size of a pony. Its hideous mandibles extended towards them and its long body extended behind it. It clicked its mouth pincer menacingly and glowered at them with its red eyes.

CHAPTER NINE
NIGHT CRAWLER

The giant millipede scuttled towards them. Its armoured back glistened in the moonlight and its many claws rattled on the wood of the pier.

'What in the name of all that's holy is that thing?' Georgia said, shivering.

'Shut up and shoot it!' Dakkar said.

'I can't,' Georgia groaned. 'I never reloaded my gun after I fired it in the courthouse!'

'It's getting closer!' Fletcher said, scrambling up on to the pile of bales.

Dakkar scanned around the deck of the pier and saw a long boat hook lying a few feet away. He lunged for it as the millipede clattered forward. Its jaws swung down towards him.

The creature's head thudded into the boards of the floor as Dakkar grabbed the pole. Georgia had found a thick length of rope, knotted at one end. She swung it slowly, waiting for the creature to come her way.

Dakkar jumped to his feet and spun round, jabbing at the millipede. It parried the blow with a vicious swipe of its mouth pincers, numbing Dakkar's arm. Georgia swung the rope in a high arc and brought it down on the millipede's head.

The creature clacked angrily and turned towards her. Georgia was defenceless as she reeled the rope in and the millipede snapped at her.

With a yell, Dakkar rammed the iron hook at its head, knocking it to one side so that its pincers sank harmlessly into the bale.

Seeing his chance, Fletcher leapt down, grabbing its tail and throwing all his weight on to it so that the millipede couldn't free itself from the bale. 'Quickly, Dakkar, finish it off!' he shouted.

Dakkar stabbed at the millipede's eyes with the spiked pole and was rewarded with a disgusting squelch as the hook sank in. Black blood splattered up the pole and the creature began to thrash about.

Fletcher gave a yell and sailed through the air as the millipede wrenched itself free. He landed with a heavy thud on the planks of the pier and groaned in pain. The creature rounded on him as he lay helpless.

'Don't worry, Fletcher,' Georgia gasped and swung her rope around the millipede's tail end. She grabbed the other end of the rope and pulled, dragging the tail back. Dakkar leapt up on to it, fearfully aware that

Georgia was struggling to keep it still. The millipede had gripped one of Fletcher's arms in its mouth and was slowly crushing it. Dakkar stood, wobbling on the shiny carapace. Georgia's feet slid along the damp floor.

Gripping the pole with both hands, Dakkar gave a yell and brought the sharp spike down on the millipede's head. The spike punched into the armour and sank deep into the creature. Something wet splattered on Dakkar's cheek and he grimaced. The millipede began to thrash about, hammering its legs on the deck of the pier and bucking up and down.

Dakkar threw himself off the millipede's back, rolling away as he landed. Georgia let go of the tail, as the millipede twisted and writhed in its death throes. Fletcher freed his arm and scurried away. With one final arch of its body, the millipede lay still.

For a second all was silent on the pier. Then a dreadful moaning arose from the ship. The crew of the *Serqet* lined its deck and glared at Dakkar.

Georgia had dragged Fletcher to his feet. 'We'd better get out of here, Dakkar, now!' she yelled.

Dakkar nodded and began backing away from the ship. One by one, the crew began to edge down the gangplank.

A large man wearing a red turban appeared on the main deck. He gave a shout and said something in Turkish to his men. The crew stopped advancing but kept their swords held high. Some of them grabbed the body of the millipede and manhandled it on board.

'Forgive me, my prince,' the man said in English. 'I would dearly love to spend more time making your acquaintance but my orders are not to get involved in a direct fight with you. So I'll bid you farewell, for now!'

'Who are you?' Dakkar demanded. He took a step forward but the crewmen who stood on the pier gave a growl and raised their weapons. 'Whose orders?'

'I think you know that already,' the man said, holding his arms open wide. He wore robes and a curved sword like the scimitar Dakkar had taken on the pirate ship. The man smiled but Dakkar could see hatred in his eyes. 'You thought you could defeat Cryptos but revenge is ours. And how sweet it is. You will remain trapped in this city, a fugitive from the very people you tried to protect. One day, they will hang you for a murderer. You could try to follow us but who would help you do that? Without your precious Commander Blizzard or Count Oginski, you are a weakling child.'

He said something in his own language and the crew began to back away from Dakkar and those aboard returned to preparing to sail. Men threw ropes from the pier on to the ship and then leapt aboard. More men in smaller boats began rowing and pulling the ship out into the river. Dakkar watched as the man on the main deck grew smaller and smaller. Finally he heard the man's last words drifting over the water.

'Good luck, Prince Dakkar! Stay and hang for a murder you didn't commit or follow us and die.'

The ship vanished into the night, and the man's mocking laughter faded with it.

'I have to go after them,' Dakkar said, punching his fist into his palm.

'But how?' Georgia said, still holding Fletcher, who leaned against her, dazed. 'You heard the man. He's right. Who is going to help you? You're wanted for murder!'

'I need to get to the *Nautilus*,' Dakkar said. 'There's more at stake than just my innocence now. Cryptos are up to something and they've gone to great efforts to neutralise us. We have to find out what they're up to and stop them.'

'What's that?' Fletcher groaned, struggling to his feet and nursing his injured arm. 'Stopping Cryptos? The *Nautilus*?'

'You know it'll be guarded,' Georgia said. 'What are your chances of getting it without a fight?'

'Practically nil,' Dakkar admitted.

'Then let's go and get her,' Georgia said with a grin.

The high wall surrounding the naval dockyard cast a deep shadow over Dakkar, Georgia and Fletcher as they crept towards the main gate, making them almost invisible. Three guards stood warming their hands over a brazier, cursing the weather.

Fletcher stepped out into the glow of the fire, giving the men a start. They leapt back, and one levelled his rifle.

'Blimey, where'd you spring from?' the rifle guard said.

'Sorry, chaps,' Fletcher said. 'Just wanted to warm meself for a moment . . .' Fletcher extended his hands over the flames and Dakkar saw the paper rolls fall into the brazier.

Any moment . . . NOW! he thought.

Fletcher threw himself backward as a loud bang erupted from the fire, sending sparks and ashes into the faces of the men huddled around it.

Dakkar leapt into the firelight, kicking one guard firmly in the head. He crumpled like a puppet whose strings have been cut. Georgia rapped another guard with her pistol and Fletcher wrestled the last one to the ground and knocked him out.

They stood panting for a moment, then Dakkar hurried through the gate. 'No time to waste,' he said, leading the others. 'That bang will bring more guards, I'm sure of it.'

He looked over to the boat shed that housed the *Nautilus*. It lay dark and silent. No sign of any other guards.

'It's remarkably quiet,' Georgia commented as they ran.

They crossed the yard to the boat shed, keeping low and sprinting between piles of planking and rowing boats laid out for repair. At last they got to the shed and pushed on the thick wooden door. It opened with a creak that made Dakkar wince.

The deep blackness inside prevented Dakkar from seeing anything. He knew that the shed covered a deep channel that led into the river. The *Nautilus* sat in this channel, waiting to go out to sea again.

A flame lit up the shed. Dakkar glimpsed the light on the water, the polished planks and brass of the *Nautilus*, an oil lamp sparking to life, the face of James Clark-Ross and the barrel of a musket pointed directly at him.

CHAPTER TEN
PERSUASION

More lamps flared in the boat shed, casting huge shadows on the wooden walls and flickering on the water. James Clark-Ross looked pale and unhappy. A number of guards stood with rifles raised and pointed at Dakkar.

'James, you have to let us go,' Dakkar said. 'The real killer is escaping as we speak.'

Clark-Ross lifted a hand for silence. 'Dashed awkward but I can't. Not after –'

'James, are you listening?' Georgia said. 'Dakkar is innocent and he can prove it if you just give him a chance!'

Clark-Ross frowned. 'What are you talking about?'

'We went to investigate the *Serqet*. The captain of the ship virtually admitted that it was one of his men who killed Chudwell, just to disgrace me!' Dakkar said. He took a step forward and the guards twitched their rifles.

'I'd keep still if I were you, Dakkar,' Clark-Ross said.

ll not have any tricks played on me. Why would anyone want to disgrace you?'

'Trust me, James, Cryptos are trying to put me out of the fight,' Dakkar replied. 'The name "Serqet" refers to an Ancient Egyptian scorpion goddess. The knife that killed Chudwell had a scorpion dagger. All the crew had scorpion tattoos and similar daggers themselves, like on the pirate ship. You have to get word to Blizzard that Cryptos are on the move . . .'

'And they're getting away while we chinwag here!' Fletcher said, exasperated. A few of the guards shifted nervously and glanced at each other.

James pursed his lips and glanced at his guards. 'I'm not sure,' he said.

'I am,' Fletcher said, springing forward, pulling the scorpion dagger from his belt and holding it to James's throat. 'I brought this along as evidence but time's running out. I think your guards will throw their guns into the water and then go and wait by the door while we climb aboard the *Nautilus* . . .'

James glanced at his men, who stared back, licking the sweat from their top lips and slowly lowering their rifles. 'You'd never do it,' he said, but his voice faltered.

'You don't know me, sir,' Fletcher growled, pressing the edge a little harder to James's throat. 'I grew up hard in the St Giles slums, fought wiv Commander Blizzard on HMS *Slaughter*. Life's cheap to me.'

James looked sadly at Dakkar. 'Why didn't you just stay in the courtroom? We could have avoided all this unpleasantness. Now you're a wanted man for sure. You and your friends.'

'I'm sorry, James,' Dakkar said. 'But I'm not going to be hanged for something I didn't do. Not when there's a chance I can prove my innocence. Now, are you going to tell your men to stand down?'

James gave a sigh. 'Very well,' he said. 'Throw your guns down, men.'

'You heard the officer, boys,' Georgia said, grabbing one guard by the arm. 'In fact, no. You give me your rifle. The rest of you, throw them in the water and make for the door . . .'

Quickly the men did as they were told. The guards shuffled away towards the door.

'Dakkar, don't do this,' James pleaded. 'If this *is* some kind of plan to ruin your good name, then you're playing right into their hands!'

'If that's the only way to sort it out and stop Cryptos,' Dakkar said coldly, unmooring the submersible, 'then so be it.'

He and Georgia climbed on to the deck of the *Nautilus* while Fletcher backed cautiously along the gangplank.

'You won't get away with this,' James said.

'I think we just 'ave, sir,' Fletcher replied, giving James a hard shove and sending him splashing into the water.

'I'm sorry that you had to get wet,' Dakkar said as James surfaced, spluttering and coughing up the river.

He clambered up the main tower of the submarine and climbed inside. It felt good to be back in the *Nautilus*.

Fletcher sealed the hatch in the top of the tower and climbed down to join Georgia and Dakkar in the control room. Dakkar sank into the captain's chair.

'Now let's get going,' he muttered.

'You reckon we can catch them?' Fletcher said.

'We could,' Dakkar said. He turned the brass handle in the wall of the control room and slowly the *Nautilus* began to sink.

'But we aren't going to, are we?' Georgia said, raising one eyebrow at Dakkar's reflection in the viewing window that filled the front wall of the tower.

'Not going to catch them?' Fletcher said, scratching his head as the dark waters enveloped them and rose up against the windows.

'This is all part of a bigger plot,' Dakkar said. 'And if Cryptos are involved, I think the *Serqet* will lead us straight to another Oginski. I can clear my name in good time. Stopping Cryptos from committing some terrible atrocity is our priority now.' Dakkar looked out into the filthy waters of the Thames. He could see James treading water above him and felt a twinge of guilt, but also relief that he was unhurt. 'All we have to do now is to get out to sea.'

'That could be tricky,' Fletcher said, peering into the murky waters of the Thames. He looked at the glowing balls of glass attached to the sides of the sub. 'What *are* those things that light our way? They give me the creeps.'

'They're just luminous jellyfish,' Dakkar said. 'There are holes in the glass so the jellyfish can still feed but they keep the way lit.'

'I think it's pretty,' Georgia said. Then she gave a shudder. 'The light, I mean, not what it shows up!'

Even with this source of light, it was like inching through a thick fog. Silt, sewage, old rope and sails, carcasses of dead animals all drifted along the riverbed, making travel difficult.

'Why don't we just sail on the surface?' Fletcher said, staring out over Dakkar's shoulder and wiping the sweat from his brow.

Dakkar smiled. 'The Thames is busy, even at this time of night. If we surface at the wrong time, we could be hit by another ship.'

'We might lose the *Serqet*,' Georgia said, gripping the back of Dakkar's seat.

'We can travel faster than her,' Dakkar said. 'I suggest we make full speed to the mouth of the river and wait for her to come to us. Then we can follow her.'

'You make it sound simple,' Georgia said, wincing as a half-sunk rowing boat bumped and scraped along their hull.

'Well, it isn't. But you're in good hands,' Dakkar said. 'I've only ever sunk a submersible once . . .'

'Twice,' Georgia corrected.

'All right then, twice,' Dakkar said, grinning at her.

They inched their way along the bed of the Thames, giving bursts of speed whenever possible. Travelling deep under the water, they weren't sure when they passed the *Serqet*, but eventually they reached the sea and surfaced.

'Now we wait,' Dakkar said and hurried up the ladder.

Dakkar sat on the tower of the *Nautilus*, gulping in the fresh sea air. Georgia joined him.

'Glad to be back out on the water?' she asked.

Dakkar nodded. 'Out here, I feel free,' he asked. 'The sea belongs to nobody and nobody rules it.'

'Nemo,' Georgia said.

'What?'

'Isn't that what "Nemo" means? Nobody or no man? That's what Blizzard told me.' Georgia gave a cough and tried an impersonation of the commander: 'Nemo, my girl, means "No Man". We are nobodies, pledged to protect the nation. In secret, unknown. No thanks given, no reward expected. That's the essence of Project Nemo, girl!' She gave Dakkar a wink.

Dakkar smiled. 'Sometimes I wish I was nobody. With no responsibilities, no enemies.'

'If wishes were fishes.' Georgia grinned.

'You're talking nonsense,' Dakkar said.

'If wishes were fishes, we'd cast nets in the sea,' she said, finishing the saying. 'It's easy to wish, Dakkar, but wishes aren't real. You have to make things happen by doing something. We can't run away from our problems; we have to face them.'

'I know we do, but I could easily run away,' Dakkar said, staring down at the waves. 'I could live down there, away from everybody. Maybe one day I will.'

'And what about us?' Georgia said gently. 'Your friends?'

Dakkar shook himself. 'You could come with me!'

'Well, don't go diving away just yet, Captain Nemo,' Georgia said, pointing at some distant lights in the darkness. 'I think our ship has come in!'

CHAPTER ELEVEN

DRAGGED TO THE DEPTHS

The *Serqet* drifted past them, oblivious to the fact that they floated just a hundred yards or so below the water.

'What shall we do?' Fletcher murmured, watching the dim black outline of the hull in the distance. 'We could sink her . . .'

'And where would that leave us?' Dakkar snorted. 'We're after Cryptos, remember? No, we must follow them, closely but without being detected.'

'We can keep below the surface most of the time but we will have to come up every now and then,' Georgia said, starting the *Nautilus*'s engines. 'If we hang back beyond view, we'll be able to do that when we need to.'

Following the *Serqet* and keeping hidden from other ships made the journey along the Channel pass quicker than Dakkar remembered it. One dull, overcast evening, Dakkar stood in the tower of the submersible, letting the cold breeze tear through his thick, black hair.

'Last time I sailed the Mediterranean, I had Count Oginski in a critical condition and the *Nautilus* was letting in water,' Dakkar said to Georgia.

He fell silent. Oginsksi had been like a father to him. And now he was gone, killed by his own brothers who ran the evil Cryptos organisation. Dakkar sighed.

The Cornish coastline lay distant and grey to his right. He stared at the far-off cliffs.

'I used to live there,' he said.

'Do you miss it?' Georgia asked.

Dakkar shrugged. 'It was my home from when I was ten,' he said. 'But I could never go back there. Too many bad memories.'

The castle was rather grandly named, given it was really a single tower at the top of the cliffs with outhouses huddled around its base. But it had been Dakkar's and Oginski's refuge until Cryptos razed it to the ground.

'Do you ever think of going to your other home?' Georgia said. 'Back to India?'

Dakkar shook his head. 'If I went back to my father's kingdom, what would I tell him?' he said. 'That I have completed my education? And what if Cryptos followed me there? I would put my family, my whole people at risk. No, I can't go home . . .'

'Not until Cryptos is finished,' Georgia said, speaking Dakkar's thoughts out loud.

'I thought I could avoid them but it seems that I've got to fight this battle to the end,' Dakkar said. 'I didn't even choose to get involved. I just got caught up in it.'

Georgia put a hand on Dakkar's arm. 'I think we all got tangled in Cryptos's web,' she said. 'But if we can get to the bottom of this, clear your name, find out why Cryptos are building this army, maybe we can solve it once and for all.'

'I hope so,' Dakkar murmured, looking out at the grey line of land. 'We've got to.'

The pursuit continued, the *Serqet*'s sails a stack of distant off-white squares against the grey sky. The land vanished behind them and Dakkar kept the *Nautilus* beneath the waves as much as he could.

Four days into their journey, Dakkar stood trailing fishing lines from the deck with Georgia, while Fletcher steered the vessel.

Georgia gave an impatient sigh. 'It's so frustrating, just sneaking along behind this darned ship! I almost wish they'd spot us. I want some action!'

Dakkar grinned. 'Me too, but we have to be cautious. We know the *Serqet* is heading for the Mediterranean just from its course,' he said, jiggling the line he held in his hands. 'We don't know where she's heading after she passes the Strait of Gibraltar.'

'I know, I know,' Georgia said.

The sound of a distant bell drifted across the waves. Dakkar frowned and squinted at the *Serqet*. She was a tiny speck on the horizon. 'That must be an alarm bell for it to be so loud,' he muttered. 'Better get below, just in case.'

Georgia shielded her eyes with her hand and peered at the distant ship. 'Do you think they spotted us?'

'Who knows?' Dakkar said. 'But I don't want to take any chances.'

He turned to climb down into the *Nautilus* but the water at the edge of the craft boiled and something long and sinuous slithered out and up the side. Dakkar glimpsed a yellow, staring eye and a snapping beak.

'Georgia, look out . . .' he began to shout but the long tentacle wrapped around Georgia's waist and hoisted her up into the air and off the *Nautilus*.

Dakkar watched helplessly as Georgia vanished beneath the water. Another tentacle curled around the tower of the *Nautilus* towards him and Dakkar realised with horror that he was defenceless. He had left all his weapons down below in the belly of the submersible. He leaned against the wall of the tower and kicked out at the tentacle as it searched blindly for him. 'Fletcher!' he yelled.

Fletcher appeared from below, throwing Dakkar his scimitar just in time. 'Dakkar! Here!'

Dakkar caught the scimitar and brought the blade slicing down on the tentacle, cutting it in two. The writhing arm pulled back but another replaced it. Dakkar swung the sword again and hacked into the creature's arm. Two more slid up and then he caught sight of Georgia, hanging limp in the creature's grasp.

With a cry, he leapt from the tower and on to the deck of the *Nautilus*. He gripped the sword with two hands and slashed the tentacles, severing one completely and staining the submersible deck black with ink and blood. The monster dropped Georgia on to the deck but instantly began to grope for her again. Dakkar lunged forward and brought his blade slicing down. Georgia looked so still. Dakkar caught his breath. He couldn't tell if she was alive.

The squid slid back into the sea and Dakkar tried to drag Georgia to the tower, but as he neared it the water exploded again, sending them both crashing to the deck. The squid had returned, agonised and furious. It swung its tentacles down at them and Dakkar barely had a chance to roll out of the way. He jumped to his feet and hacked at two tentacles that wrapped around his lower legs.

Georgia revived and clutched her stomach, coughing up seawater. 'I have an idea,' she gasped.

Fletcher had reloaded and fired a rifle ball straight into the creature's huge eye. He couldn't miss and the squid made a strange squealing sound, slithering a tentacle up the tower towards him.

Georgia staggered the length of the deck before scrambling up the ladder, kicking away a tentacle that snagged her leg, trying to drag her off. She fell over the low wall that protected the top of the tower and crawled down into the ship.

'Georgia, what are you doing?' Fletcher bellowed, jabbing at the attacking tentacle with the bayonet fixed on his rifle. Dakkar cut and hacked at the rubbery arms as they tried to tighten around him.

Georgia reappeared at the top of the tower, gripping a

huge rifle with a massive barrel. It took both hands to heft the gun on to the side of the tower. She pulled back the hammer and pointed the rifle at the squid.

The gunshot was deafening. For a second a high-pitched ringing filled Dakkar's ears. An explosion of blood and tissue erupted across them. Georgia stood, still gripping the massive gun. The squid thrashed around, a huge chunk blown from its head. Blood washed the deck of the *Nautilus*. Dakkar ran to the tower, dodging the tentacles that lashed to and fro in the squid's death throes.

'A punt gun!' Georgia shouted, partly from her own deafness and partly in victory. 'They use them to shoot whole braces of ducks at a time. Thought it'd be useful one day!'

'It's like a small cannon!' Fletcher groaned, still covering his ears with his hands.

The water bubbled black and bloody around the *Nautilus* as the squid slowly sank back to the depths.

Dakkar looked up and scanned the horizon. The *Serqet* had vanished.

CHAPTER TWELVE

IBRAHIM

Ignoring his aches and bruises, Dakkar hurried to the controls of the *Nautilus* and sent her hurtling after the *Serqet*.

'They must have spotted us and unleashed that kraken,' he said. 'We can't afford to lose her.'

'Where do they keep them?' Fletcher wondered aloud.

'From what I've seen in the past, they seem to store them in cages under the ship,' Georgia said, watching the bubbles boil around the windows as they submerged. 'They release them when they need to. Like that beast on the pirate ship.'

'Let's just hope they haven't got any more monsters in store,' Dakkar said. 'If we ever catch up with them.'

It took two days for them to locate the *Serqet* again, weaving back and forth, retracing their steps. Finally they went through the Strait of Gibraltar and into the Mediterranean Sea. Shipping was busy here and they had to remain submerged for long hours, which made them hot and irritable in the stuffy cabins.

Finally, Fletcher spotted the *Serqet* a few miles from the North African coast.

'It looks like she's heading for Algiers,' Georgia said, consulting the sea charts.

The *Serqet* sailed into the harbour of Algiers but Dakkar held back. Several fortified islands stretched in front of the port like a letter 'T' from the shore and the buildings of the main city.

'Can you see any cannon?' he said, passing the telescope to Georgia. At the centre of the 'T' was a large fort, bristling with guns just ready to blow anything slightly suspicious to pieces.

'We could go under the ships,' Fletcher suggested but Dakkar shook his head.

'No,' he said. 'Look at all the masts; the place is full of ships. We'd never find somewhere to dock secretly. I think we're going to have to moor down the coast a little and travel back to the port by land.'

'It is a risk, though,' Georgia said. 'We don't know what kind of reception we'll get there. The people of Algiers aren't friends to Europeans or Americans.'

'We can always disguise ourselves,' Dakkar said. 'We have some heavy robes in the trunk down below.'

They steered the *Nautilus* to a secluded, rocky bay where lonely seagull cries echoed from the cliffs.

'The *Nautilus* should be safe enough here,' Dakkar said as he clambered out after securing her ropes to the shore.

They'd dressed in long robes that had been sitting in the hold of the submarine. Dakkar's mentor, the late Count Oginski, had put them there in case they were needed for desert travel.

'These smell awful!' Georgia said with a grimace.

Dakkar shrugged. 'They've been in the hold for a long time,' he said. 'Anyway I quite like them. I've dressed like an Englishman since I was ten!'

'You look like a proper Barbary pirate now,' Fletcher said, grinning. Dakkar gave him a reproving look.

'I'm from India, Fletcher, not the North of Africa,' he said, raising an eyebrow.

'Sorry, sir,' Fletcher began, but a footstep rattling on the shingle behind them cut him short. They all turned to see a shadowy figure darting between the rocks.

The figure ducked behind a nearby boulder. Dakkar could just see a ragged elbow poking out from the stone. He stepped forward, drawing his sharp scimitar while Fletcher pulled a pistol from his belt.

'You'd better come out unless you want me to start waving this sword about,' Dakkar said in imperfect Turkish.

A small, serious-eyed boy emerged from behind the boulder. Dakkar thought he couldn't have been more than eight years old. The boy's clothes were ragged and torn and his hair hung matted and tangled around his dirt-smudged face. He fell to his knees before Dakkar.

'Mercy, master, don't cut my head off!' he sobbed, gripping Dakkar's ankles.

'Really, there's no . . .' Dakkar began, but before he could finish the boy had rolled under his legs and sent him sprawling, before leaping forward and snatching the pistol from Fletcher's hand.

He stood, panting and grinning. 'Now, you dog,' he said, waving the pistol. 'Your purse, if you please!'

Dakkar grinned. Georgia emerged from the tower and stood behind the boy, rifle pointed right at his head.

'I suggest you give the pistol back before my friend blows what few brains you have all over this beach,' Dakkar said, raising his eyebrows.

The boy looked over his shoulder and then scowled, uncocking the pistol and handing it back to Fletcher.

'I've a good mind to put you over my knee!' Georgia said, climbing down and stomping over the shingle towards the boy.

The boy scowled at Georgia. 'What did she say?' he said. 'I don't like her. She looks all angry.'

Dakkar laughed. He couldn't help liking the boy. 'She wants to beat you. What's your name?'

The boy's eyes widened. 'My name is Ibrahim. Keep the angry girl away from me!'

'What did he say?' Georgia said, narrowing her eyes at Ibrahim.

'He likes you.' Dakkar smirked.

'Blimey, Dakkar, where d'you learn that lingo from?' Fletcher said, staring at Dakkar in admiration.

'My father made sure I knew all the languages of the major countries and empires,' Dakkar said. 'Keep still!'

The boy had started to edge away from them. Now his face crumpled again, but this time he seemed more genuine. 'Please, master, don't kill me! I am a poor boy with no father, or mother, have pity on me!'

Dakkar looked hard at the boy. 'Kill you? I am Prince Dakkar of Bundelkhand,' he said, raising his chin and trying to sound as haughty and pompous as possible. 'I would not sully my hands with the blood of a mere child! But what to do with you? That is the question . . .'

Ibrahim stood, eyes wide as Dakkar paced back and forth.

He turned and pointed at Ibrahim. 'You threatened the royal personage! You called me a dog!'

'I wouldn't have actually shot you, master. Especially if you'd handed over your purse!' Ibrahim's eyes widened even more, if that were possible. 'Besides, there have been so many strange happenings, strange people and . . . and . . . monstrosities, I really wouldn't have known you were a prince of the blood!'

'What's he saying now?' Georgia snapped, making Ibrahim flinch.

'Monstrosities?' Dakkar said slowly, ignoring Georgia. 'What do you mean?'

'Hideous creatures, spiders the size of sheep!' Ibrahim said, falling to his knees again. 'Armies of strange men.'

'What do they look like?' Dakkar said.

'Fierce warriors. Mad-eyed and ruthless . . .'

'Did they have any . . . marks on them?'

'Yes, master,' Ibrahim said, sounding surprised that

Dakkar knew. 'The mark of a scorpion, drawn on their bodies. Some of them landed boats here and carried cargo, cages of these hideous monsters . . .'

'Where did they go?'

'To the south,' Ibrahim said. 'Deep into the desert, so the rumours say.'

Dakkar smiled. 'Well, Ibrahim, I've thought of a way you can redeem yourself!'

Relief washed over Ibrahim's face. 'Anything, master,' he said, bowing far too many times.

'You've let him off?' Georgia said.

'He's only a boy,' Fletcher murmured. 'What harm can he do?'

'He can help us,' Dakkar said. 'But only if you're his special friend.'

Georgia looked appalled. 'I hate little kids, and he tried to murder you!'

'He tried to rob me,' Dakkar corrected him. He nodded over to Fletcher. 'What do you think, Fletcher? He's a poor boy, trying to get by. Says he's lost his father and mother.'

Fletcher grinned. 'Sounds like he's got potential! Give him a chance, I say!' Fletcher winked at Ibrahim, who winked back and grinned.

'I like him,' Ibrahim said. 'He looks like a friend.'

'He is, Ibrahim,' Dakkar said. 'Just so long as you don't let us down.'

'I won't, master,' Ibrahim said, leaping to his feet. 'Just say what you want and Ibrahim will make it happen. I have many friends all over Algiers!'

'I need a map and a guide to where the scorpion men went,' Dakkar said. Ibrahim's face paled.

'I can get you fresh fruit, water, a camel!' Ibrahim said, wringing his hands. 'But nobody will go after those devils!'

'Yes, an apple would be nice,' Dakkar said. 'Get me an apple too.' He turned to Georgia. 'Do you want an apple?'

'What?' Georgia said, glancing between Ibrahim and Dakkar in confusion.

'I'd like an apple,' Fletcher said.

Dakkar turned back to Ibrahim. 'You're making the angry girl cross,' Dakkar said to him. 'She wants an apple too. *And* someone to guide us south.'

Ibrahim edged back from Georgia. 'I can get you apples,' he said, eyeing her and tangling his fingers together. 'But I'm more afraid of the scorpion men than of her!'

'He still likes you,' Dakkar said to Georgia, with a smile. 'Look, Ibrahim, all I want you to do is find us someone who can show us the way south. We'll pay them well and you too. You can run then. Agreed?'

Ibrahim looked relieved and nodded. 'You'd better wait here,' he said and gave Georgia one last careful glance. 'She's an angry monster,' he said and ran off.

'He says you look kind,' Dakkar said to Georgia, who shrugged. Dakkar called after him. 'And if you don't come back, the angry girl will come looking for you!'

'Have no fear, master,' Ibrahim called back. 'I will return!'

With the right kind of people, I hope, Dakkar thought, beginning to wonder if he could trust the little boy.

CHAPTER THIRTEEN
DESERT FLIGHT

They sat waiting in the rocky cove. There was little conversation. Dakkar wondered about Ibrahim again. Maybe he'd just run off; maybe he'd gone to the city and summoned the local militia; or worse, maybe right now he was telling the crew of the *Serqet* where Dakkar was. He found it hard to sit still and paced from rock to rock, continuously sitting and standing. Above them, grey clouds still blotted out the sun but it was warm, making it humid and uncomfortable.

'A year without summer,' Dakkar murmured. 'That's what Commander Blizzard said would happen.'

'Oh … yes,' Fletcher said, frowning. 'But how would he have known that then?'

'Marek Oginski blew up a volcano in the Far East, Mount Tambora,' Dakkar explained. 'Blizzard told me that the ash and smoke thrown up into the clouds would blot out the sun and cause crops to fail. There'd be famine and then rioting. Cryptos would use the chaos to further their plans.'

'And it looks like that's just what they're doing,' Georgia said. 'Gathering an army of poor, hungry soldiers in London. Getting ready to strike.'

'Not if we can help it,' Dakkar said.

More time crept slowly by.

'Do you think we can trust that boy?' Georgia said, rubbing her hands.

'I hope so,' Dakkar said. 'We need some kind of map and some local knowledge to guide us. I can't be sure, though. Ibrahim might not return at all!'

'Well, well,' Georgia said. 'Looks like your trust in the little varmint paid off.'

Ibrahim returned with four men marching behind him. They stood in a line in front of Dakkar. They looked ragged, in sun-bleached turbans and tattered robes, but Dakkar could see muscle under their rags and steel in their eyes.

Ibrahim bowed. 'I bring you four fierce warriors for inspection, your highness,' he said. 'I told them that you were a mighty potentate from the East.' He came closer and whispered. 'I told them you were a fierce warrior and had much gold too. They speak good English, having fought all over the world in the Dey's navy . . .'

'Having begged in the port of Algiers more like, you little monkey,' the biggest of the men said.

'Speak for yourself, peasant!' another said. He looked older than the others, his beard showing flecks of silver.

He stood slightly apart from them and had a rifle slung over his back. 'I have fought for the Dey himself and learned many languages in his palace . . .'

'I managed to get this too,' Ibrahim said, ignoring them. He handed Dakkar a rolled-up map.

The first man bowed. He looked well groomed, his long black beard clean and combed. 'Karim, your highness,' he said, smiling. 'I am proficient in all weapons but I favour a sword and dagger.'

'Mourad,' the man who had called Ibrahim a monkey said, scowling. He seemed the opposite of Karim, giant and wide, more muscular and unkempt. 'I have the strength of three men. At your service.'

'Forgive this uncultured peasant, your greatness,' the third man said, grinning and giving Mourad a dig with his elbow. 'He doesn't know how to conduct himself in front of royalty. I am Yunus, the best knife-thrower and hand-to-hand fighter in Algiers. It's an honour to serve.'

Dakkar smirked. He could see the stocky Mourad glowering at Yunus.

The final one to speak was the older man. He gave a low bow. 'My name is Zaki, your highness,' he said. 'Veteran of the Dey's personal guard. There is nobody who can shoot better than I.'

Dakkar glanced at Georgia, who was the best marksman Dakkar knew. She smiled back serenely, not rising to Dakkar's silent challenge.

'Zaki can shoot a fly off a camel's backside and not hurt the camel,' Yunus said excitedly.

'I found them at the local market,' Ibrahim muttered with an embarrassed cough, 'guarding the merchants' goods. They've been hired to keep the scorpion men from raiding the camel trains. Times are hard, your highness. Money is scarce.'

'Excellent, Ibrahim,' Dakkar said, beaming. 'You've served me well.' He turned to the men. 'You know where we want to go?'

'South,' Zaki said. 'To the Temple of Serqet . . .'

'Is that where the men with the scorpion tattoos come from?' Dakkar said.

Mourad stepped forward. 'They do,' he said. 'Recently they have spread great misery around here. Terrorising womenfolk and taking food and provisions. The Dey, our great ruler, seems powerless to stop them.'

'The men worship the scorpion goddess,' Karim murmured. 'They control these terrible beasts with some kind of sorcery. They are evil and we would stop them to protect our kinfolk.'

'Then you know that this is a dangerous mission,' Dakkar said. 'I cannot promise your safety but I can promise you a rich reward once we reach this temple.' He tossed each man a gold coin and their eyes widened.

Dakkar looked at them. He didn't know if he could trust them entirely but they seemed to want to stop the trouble being caused by the scorpion men. 'Now, gentlemen, are you ready for the adventure of your lives?'

The men nodded. 'I am ready to die for you, your highness,' Yunus declared.

'Hopefully that won't be necessary,' Dakkar said. 'This is Miss Georgia Fulton and this is Mr Fletcher. They are my sworn allies and friends. Treat them as you would treat me. Now, follow us. Our adventure begins!'

'But, your highness,' Zaki stammered. 'We have no camels or donkeys. How will we travel?'

'Behold,' Dakkar waved a theatrical hand to the *Nautilus*, which bobbed on the waves close by. He led them over to it and hauled on the rope to bring it closer to shore.

The men eyed the *Nautilus* warily and huddled together on the rocks as Dakkar leapt on to the deck.

'What devilry is this?' Zaki said, pacing the shore alongside the submersible and inspecting the glistening planks.

'It is a ship of some kind,' Mourad said, running his fingers through his thick wiry hair.

Yunus laughed. 'Mourad, you're a genius! A wooden structure floating on the water,' he said, digging the huge Mourad in the ribs with his elbow. 'How did you guess?'

Mourad opened his mouth to say something but Karim interrupted him. 'It is a covered boat,' Karim said, realisation dawning on him. 'Is it possible? Your highness, does it travel under the waves?'

'Under the waves?' Zaki snorted. 'Karim, have you lost your senses? Do you think he has a flying carpet inside too?'

Dakkar stood on the deck and threw his arms wide in

another theatrical gesture. 'This, gentlemen, is the *Nautilus*,' he said. 'She travels under the sea and over the land.'

Zaki's eyes widened. 'It flies? Then you do have a magic carpet?'

This time it was Karim's turn to smile. 'Hot-air balloons is my guess,' he said. 'I once saw a Frenchman fly a balloon over the pyramids in Egypt. But that balloon was huge and carried only one man in a basket. How could such a huge craft fly?'

'Why don't we get on board and find out?' Georgia said. Dakkar detected a hint of suspicion in her voice.

Dakkar turned to Ibrahim and pushed two gold coins into his hand. 'Ibrahim, thank you,' he said. 'Our paths part here.'

'I could come with you, master,' Ibrahim said. 'I have no family to keep me here, and you have lots of gold. Maybe I could help you again!'

Dakkar grinned. 'Alas, Ibrahim. I'd love to take you along but it is too dangerous.'

He gave Ibrahim one last smile and hurried after Fletcher, who had already gone inside. Behind them, the wary men clambered down the ladder into the control room of the submersible. Their amazement grew as they stared at the brass levers and wheels that studded the wall in front of Dakkar's seat.

Dakkar held the wheel of the *Nautilus*. 'We haven't time for a demonstration of the ship's underwater capabilities, but hold on tight because we're going to be airborne in a few minutes.'

With a grin at Fletcher and Georgia, Dakkar reached down, pulling a lever at his right foot. The pipes that snaked around the control room hissed to life, making the men jump. Zaki reached for his sword.

'It sounds like a thousand snakes,' Mourad gasped.

'It is merely gas and hot air inflating the balloons,' Dakkar said, smiling. 'Look through the windows.'

The balloons of white silk were blossoming from their casings and rising up, trailing ropes that soon became taut.

'In a moment, we'll lift up off the water,' Fletcher said. 'It's a funny feeling. Makes me a bit queasy, to be honest.'

'Queasy?' Yunus said.

The boat gave a jolt and the sound of water rushing off the hull filled the *Nautilus*. Dakkar felt his stomach lurch as they rose into the sky. Yunus's face went slightly grey.

Fletcher gave a laugh. 'Yeah, queasy,' he said, nodding at Yunus.

Soon they were floating high above the ground. Dakkar could see the city and its harbour off to his left, and ahead the mountains stretched away towards the desert and danger.

CHAPTER FOURTEEN
STOWAWAY

The men spent a lot of time gasping and commenting on how small everything looked. Dakkar remembered the first time he had been airborne. It hadn't been in this airship, adapted by himself and Oginski; it had been on the back of a giant flying reptile in a world deep underground. *This world holds more wonders than these men can imagine*, he thought. But the novelty of flying over the scrubby brown desert land impressed even Dakkar.

Mountains passed below them and the air grew cold. 'Not as cold as Greenland,' Fletcher said, rubbing the frozen condensation off the glass of the window. Dakkar nodded. Their last adventure against Cryptos had taken them to the frozen North. Dakkar sighed. It hadn't ended well. He shook his head, dismissing an image of his mentor, Oginski, slipping over the edge of the *Nautilus* down to the sea below.

Gradually the dark green of the foothills gave way to

brown earth and rock and ahead they could see a golden expanse of sand. Georgia looked at the chart that the Dey had given them while Fletcher held a compass. 'We're heading into the desert,' she said.

'I hope your ship can stay in the air now, your highness,' Yunus murmured, staring down at the vastness of the desert. 'Because if it can't, we will not last long down there.'

'There is an oasis to the south-west,' Karim said, ignoring him. 'The followers of Serqet have built a fortress temple around it.'

'Sounds like a fun place to go,' Fletcher said. 'And how on earth are we going to sneak up on them in this thing?'

'I suggest we land some distance away from the fortress and sneak there under cover of darkness,' Dakkar said.

'The desert is like a rolling sea of sand,' Zaki added. 'Your craft will be concealed by the sand dunes, your highness.'

'The trouble is we'll be spotted long before we've landed,' Dakkar said, squinting out of the window. 'Georgia, once we're getting close to that fortress, we need to fly low, as close to the ground as possible . . .'

'I'll go up top and keep a lookout for it,' Georgia said, understanding him straight away. 'As soon as I see it, I'll holler.' She climbed up the ladder to sit at the top of the tower and keep watch.

The landscape below became monotonous as they drifted over it. Even the sky's welcome blue after all the clouds had become oppressive. Fletcher had shown the men the cabins below and they had marvelled at the engine and the armaments. Now they fell silent, staring glumly out of the viewing window. The only sound was the steady hum of the propellers at the rear of the craft. The heat grew, making the cabin at the base of the *Nautilus*'s tower stuffy and uncomfortable.

'With all due respect, your highness,' Karim said, breaking the quiet, 'I'll be glad to step out of this craft and feel my feet on firm ground again.'

'That's only natural, Karim,' Dakkar said. 'Me? I could live in the *Nautilus* for ever but I would live beneath the waves. I do not like the skies.'

'Dax, I think you'd better come up here!' Georgia yelled from above.

Dakkar frowned and handed the controls over to Fletcher. 'What is it?' Dakkar said, squinting against the bright sunlight as he popped his head out of the tower.

Georgia said nothing but stepped to one side to reveal the small, forlorn form of Ibrahim trembling before him. 'Forgive me, master, I didn't want to be left alone. I can help. I am brave! I climbed on to the ship when it began to leave the water. I didn't know it would fly so high!'

'Ibrahim!' Dakkar hissed the name through his teeth. 'It's too dangerous!'

'He must have clung to the deck all the way here,' Georgia said. 'Tough little scrap and no mistake.'

'We should throw him overboard!' Dakkar growled. Ibrahim's eyes widened and he fell to his knees.

'Your highness, majesty, most worshipful one,' Ibrahim gabbled. 'Have mercy!'

A smirk forced its way across Dakkar's face and he caught Georgia's eye. She grinned back. 'Looks like we've got another crew member,' she said, narrowing her eyes at Ibrahim.

'On second thoughts, your majesty, throw me overboard,' Ibrahim said. 'Just don't let the scary lady kill me!'

'You get inside and don't touch anything or I'll tell her to make your life a living hell!' Dakkar said, but there was humour in his voice too. He gave Georgia a secret smile as Ibrahim scurried down into the *Nautilus*.

But Georgia's attention was focused elsewhere. 'Look, Dakkar, that square building down there. It looks like a stockade, with a lake in the middle. It must be the temple,' she said.

Dakkar frowned and squinted in the direction she was gazing. 'Our journey's end,' he said. 'We'd better start to lose height.'

'We'd better get the guns out,' Georgia whispered.

'Why? I can't see anything down there that would –'

'Look up, not down,' Georgia said, gripping his shoulder.

Dakkar squinted up into the bright sky. The silhouette of an enormous bird circled above them, blotting out the sun.

'It looks like some kind of huge vulture,' Georgia called down. 'And it's headed our way. It can only have come from the temple, as far as I can see!'

The vulture circled closer. 'It's enormous,' Dakkar gasped.

The bird's body must have been as long as two men laid toe to head. Its wings extended even further, feathers ruffling in the thermal currents that held it aloft. He could see the ugly, mottled red skin of its neck, its bald skull of a head and those glittering black eyes.

'It is a roc,' Mourad called up from below. 'A giant bird from legends of old!'

'Bring your rifles up to the tower, quickly,' Dakkar snapped. 'Be careful how you shoot. It is easy to damage the balloons and I don't want any sudden landings.'

The men climbed up to join Georgia and Dakkar. 'Stay down there for now, Fletcher,' Dakkar said. 'It'll be too crowded up here. You pilot the *Nautilus*.'

'Righto,' Fletcher said, but Dakkar could tell he wanted to come up top and help. 'Better keep an eye on that thing, though, it looks like it's about to . . .'

But Fletcher's words were drowned by the screeching cry of the vulture as it folded its wings and plummeted towards the *Nautilus*.

CHAPTER FIFTEEN
SKY BATTLE

Gunfire crackled from the tower as Yunus and the other men fired on the huge bird. Dakkar saw feathers torn away from the vulture as it increased speed. But even though some of the shots had hit their mark, the bird remained locked in its plummet towards the *Nautilus*.

'With those claws, it could tear the balloons to bits like they were paper,' Georgia said faintly.

Below, Fletcher whirled the wheel around, changing the course of the *Nautilus*. But the craft was slow to respond and began a leisurely drift to the right. The bird threw out its wings, hovering and extending its claws.

It landed with a thud on the front of the *Nautilus*. The whole craft bucked and tilted down.

Zaki toppled from the crowded tower and now clung on, desperately trying not to fall.

The vulture flapped its wings, buffeting the balloons aside and sending the *Nautilus* rocking as if it were on a choppy sea. It hopped up the deck until Dakkar could see the tiniest plumage, the scales on its long legs and the cruel curve of its shiny yellow beak. Zaki kicked and scrabbled for a foothold; Karim and Mourad gripped hold of his arms.

'Shoot,' Dakkar called, but Georgia and Yunus were loading their guns. He felt so helpless. In the sea, the *Nautilus* could veer and turn, dodging its opponents, but up here they were slow and even the weapons were useless.

With an oath, he dragged his scimitar from its sheath.

Karim and Mourad heaved Zaki up but the vulture leapt forward, sending the *Nautilus* swinging. Unbalanced, the two guards lost their grip on Zaki and he fell backward with a yell.

The vulture opened its beak wide to welcome the falling man. It clamped down on his neck and raked a talon across Zaki's back. Blood splattered across the deck as the bird tore at the unfortunate guard. Then his limp body slipped off the deck and into the void beneath them.

'Zaki!' Karim cried in horror.

'Darned evil buzzard!' Georgia spat and fired. This time the bullet hit home, sending a fountain of blood spurting up from the bird's eye. With an enraged scream, the vulture leapt up on to the tower.

Dakkar could smell the creature now, a mixture of rotten meat, bird droppings and fresh blood. He could see its matted feathers and the red of Zaki's lifeblood glistening on its beak.

The vulture pecked at Karim, who fell to the floor,

blocking the attack with his rifle. The weapon was torn from his grasp and flung over the side of the tower. Dakkar leapt forward and brought his sword clanging down on the bird's curved beak.

With a squawk of rage, it snapped at him, giving Mourad a chance to step in. To everyone's amazement, the burly man swung an arm around the vulture's lumpy red neck. The bird reared up, lifting Mourad off his feet, but the man clung on, squeezing with all his might. Blood leaked from one of the bird's eyes and now the other one bulged horribly. The vulture tried to bring its leg up to impale Mourad on its claws but Karim threw himself on to the leg and held it fast. The bird's wings flapped, smacking and battering the tower. Dust and fragments of feather filled the air. One wing clipped Yunus in the temple and sent him senseless to the ground.

'Shoot it now!' Mourad yelled, veins bulging on his forehead and sweat trickling down his contorted face.

Dakkar pulled a pistol from his belt and brought it point blank to the bird's head. He fired, enveloping them all in a cloud of smoke. The pistol jerked in his hand and the vulture gave a last squawk. Blood and brain splattered all over the tower. The vulture's wings fluttered feebly then all that could be heard was the hum of the propellers and Mourad's ragged panting as he slowly released the ruined mess of the head and neck.

Yunus groaned and staggered to his feet.

'I think we should land,' Dakkar said. 'We need to take stock and if we drift any further, I fear the enemy will spot us.' He pointed to the dark square in the sand a few miles away.

'The fortress,' Georgia said, her eyes widening.

'Let's get below,' Fletcher said.

Karim and Mourad heaved the carcass of the vulture over the side of the tower and watched as it spiralled to the earth below.

The fortress was near enough to walk to but, Dakkar hoped, far enough away for the occupants not to have noticed the battle in the air. He watched the square, mud-brick structure as they descended. Now and then he saw movement but he couldn't tell whether it was people or animals moving. Dakkar saw where the vulture had crashed to the ground and aimed for it as a landing site. He released the last of the gas in the balloons and brought the *Nautilus* gently to the ground. 'The extra heat seems to make her more buoyant,' he said, wishing he felt lighter-hearted himself. He'd seen men die in battle before but it didn't make it any easier, and the way Zaki had slipped off the deck . . . It was too much like Oginski.

'Will there be any more birds like that one?' Ibrahim asked, keeping close to Dakkar's side.

'It's possible,' Dakkar said. 'But you sneaked on board, Ibrahim. You've only yourself to blame!'

Ibrahim shrugged and looked at his feet.

'Maybe if we can find Zaki's body, we can bury him,' Karim suggested.

Dakkar nodded. 'If we can; he can't have fallen far

from here,' he said. 'But how you bury someone in these shifting sands, I don't know.' He turned to Ibrahim. 'You stay here!'

The heat on the ground seared Dakkar's face. It rained down on his head and bounced up from the scalding sands. Even the air felt hot as he breathed in.

'It's like being in a furnace,' Fletcher murmured as they climbed out after Dakkar.

'That's strange,' Dakkar said, frowning and scanning the sands.

Georgia stepped behind him, wrapping a thin cotton scarf around her head to protect her from the sun. She was fair-skinned and red-headed and burned easily. 'What is?' she said.

'I could have sworn I landed the *Nautilus* close to where the vulture fell to earth,' he said, turning a full three hundred and sixty degrees searching for the bird. 'But I can't see it at all.'

'Maybe it's over the next sand dune?' Georgia said, unconvinced herself.

'I cannot see it anywhere,' Karim called from the brow of the dune above them. 'But I can see the fortress.'

Dakkar and Georgia ran up the side of the dune, slipping in the scorching sand. The land sank away from the top of this dune, raising them above this lower, flatter terrain. The fortress stood squat and square in the middle of the area; a few palm trees and scrubby bushes fringed its walls.

'It looks like they have fortified the oasis,' Karim said. 'A clever move. If an enemy came to besiege them, then the occupants are in control of the only supply of fresh drinking water for miles around.'

'If we get our telescope, we can count guards and look for any possible ways to sneak in,' Georgia suggested, turning before Dakkar could answer.

He watched her bound down the dune. 'But where has that vulture gone?' he said.

Karim shrugged. 'Maybe it travelled on the wind as it fell, your highness.'

Dakkar bit his lip thoughtfully. 'No,' he said, gripping the handle of his scimitar, which hung at his belt. 'Something is wrong. Very wrong.'

Before Karim could reply, the whole dune began to shake. Waves of sand cascaded down its sides towards the *Nautilus* and Georgia fell, rolling down, unable to control her fall.

Fletcher, Mourad and Yunus stood frozen to the spot as the *Nautilus* tilted, its stern sinking into the sand.

Fletcher's voice drifted over the rumbling of the earth and the hissing of the moving sand. 'Dakkar, the *Nautilus* is disappearing!'

Then two huge antennae poked up out of the ground next to the *Nautilus*, followed by two bulbous eyes and sharp, snapping pincers.

Dakkar watched helplessly as the ground collapsed under his companions and they slid with the sand towards the yawning hole and the awaiting creature. And Georgia wasn't far behind them.

CHAPTER SIXTEEN
BLOOD AND SAND

Sand filled Dakkar's mouth, ears and nose. He coughed and choked, squinting in the semi-dark of the sandy tunnel he found himself in. His body ached as he tried to stand. He remembered running down the dune towards Georgia and the others. He had a vague memory of the giant beetle, dull brown, the size of a carriage and covered with spiny hairs, charging at him. Then blackness.

The tunnel stretched off into the dark, its walls made of nothing but compacted sand. Every movement brought rivers of the stuff trickling to the floor. *This place could collapse at any second*, Dakkar thought. Mourad lay a few feet across the tunnel, half buried, his eyes closed. A little further over lay the enormous carcass of the vulture, picked and chewed at.

This must be some kind of underground burrow, Dakkar thought. *The giant beetle must have dragged the bird down here. That's why I couldn't see it from the air.*

Dakkar crawled towards the half-buried guard. 'Mourad,' he said, pulling his hand gently. Mourad shifted slightly and Dakkar, eager to free him from the sand that covered his legs, pulled harder. He fell back, still holding Mourad's hands, and stared in horror. Mourad's lower half had gone. It was as if he had been neatly cut in two. The sand soaked up the blood oozing from the entrails that spilled on to the tunnel floor.

Choking back a yell of horror, Dakkar dropped Mourad's remains and crawled away to the other side of the tunnel. He glanced around but couldn't see anyone else. Sunlight filtered down into the tunnel from the opening above. Dakkar reached up, jumping to get out of the hole, but it was too high and the sides just collapsed, threatening to bury him.

A faint voice echoed from the dark tunnel. 'Prince Dakkar?'

'Karim? Is that you?' Dakkar called into the shadows. He peered down the long passage. Another light glowed in the distance. He hurried towards it and found himself standing in a deep pit, blinking in the sunlight. This proved impossible to get out of too, and Dakkar cursed as he slid back down the side of the hole, spitting out sand as he did. Two other tunnels led off this pit. Dakkar peered down each one but the bright light from the mouth of the pit made the darkness in the tunnels impenetrable.

Uncertain what to do, Dakkar inched down the nearest tunnel. He drew his scimitar, taking comfort in its weight and the solid handle. Slowly his eyes became accustomed to the twilight world. Sand trickled from the ceiling as he passed and his heart pounded at his ribs. He imagined the tunnel roof caving in, tons of dry sand filling his mouth, drowning him.

'Dakkar?' Another voice! *That was Georgia*, he thought. Dakkar hurried down the passage towards it, his blade at the ready.

More voices reached Dakkar's ears now: shouting and cursing mingled with a soft rustling and a sharp clicking sound.

Once more, the light dazzled Dakkar as he stumbled into a larger pit. The *Nautilus* leaned against one wall, nose down, its balloons draped uselessly on the floor. The massive brown beetle poked its head and half of its bulbous, spiny body out of the mouth of another tunnel. Yunus and Georgia jabbed at it with bayonet-tipped rifles, their backs to Dakkar. Fletcher lay on the ground, unmoving.

Georgia turned and her eyes widened. 'Dakkar! Thank goodness,' she gasped. 'The ground just opened up and you fell into the pit after us.'

'You get behind me and reload,' Dakkar said, jumping forward. 'I'll help Yunus keep this thing occupied!'

'Mourad is gone,' Yunus panted, stabbing at the insect's snapping mandibles. 'This monster snatched you away and then dragged him into the tunnels.'

'I know,' Dakkar said. He could feel the anger boiling inside him as he thought of poor Mourad. 'Keep fighting. We can defeat this beast.' Gripping his scimitar in both hands, Dakkar brought it down on the insect's snapping jaws.

The clang echoed across the pit as the scimitar hit the bony pincers, shearing through one of them. The blow numbed Dakkar's arm but the creature gave a high-pitched, hissing shriek and jerked away from them.

Yelling with rage, Dakkar hacked and stabbed at the beetle. He was dimly aware of Yunus beside him stabbing and lunging. Black blood oozed from the creature's many wounds as it tried to back away.

Having reloaded, Georgia leapt forward, firing her rifle directly into the beetle. The creature reared up once and then crashed to the ground. Dakkar grinned and turned to Georgia.

'Good shooting,' he said, panting for breath.

'I couldn't miss,' Georgia said, but before she could say any more another dirty brown head surged from the tunnel behind them and a second set of snapping jaws knocked her aside.

Dakkar raised his sword but the insect bit into his wrist. Pain seared through Dakkar's arm, forcing a scream from his lips. His sword clanked to the ground and he hung from the creature's jaws like a puppet.

Yunus ran forward, trying to stab at this new attacker with his bayonet, but Dakkar blocked his way. The fire in Dakkar's wrist grew hotter as the pincers crushed the bone. All he could think about was the pain.

The pit see-sawed in his vision, rocking like a ship on

the sea; he felt bile rising in his throat. Then he stared at the *Nautilus*. It looked bizarre, upended and leaning against the walls of the pit, its huge fins and propellers at the rear poking into the blue sky. But amid the agony of his crushed wrist and Yunus's shouting, Dakkar glimpsed a movement. Someone was in the *Nautilus* and was watching them through the windows of the lower cabin. *Ibrahim!* Dakkar thought. *He's still in the* Nautilus.

A high-pitched whistle stabbed Dakkar's ears, momentarily blotting out the pain of his arm and making him wince. Then a glass ball fell into the pit and smashed. A sweet perfume filled the air and the insect dropped him and stood still, antennae weaving back and forth.

Ropes rolled down the side of the pit and men with scorpion tattoos on their bare chests surrounded them, shouting and pointing spears or rifles.

A figure stood at the edge of the pit looking down. The sun silhouetted him but Dakkar could see he was a big man, with brawny arms. He glimpsed flowing red hair and a bristling beard.

'Welcome, Prince Dakkar,' the man said, and Dakkar recognised the rich tones of an Oginski. 'My mistress would like to see you.'

'Which one are you?' Dakkar spat. 'Marek or Voychek?'

The shadowy shape inclined his head. 'Names are meaningless,' he said. 'I am merely a vessel for the Holy Serqet, praise be to her!' The men around Dakkar all mumbled something in response and touched their chests. 'Bring them up!'

Dakkar, Georgia, Fletcher and Yunus were tied and hoisted out of the pit. Fletcher's eyelid flickered and a gentle groan escaped his lips. *At least he's alive!* Dakkar thought.

The man at the top of the pit had to be an Oginski. He looked very much like Franciszek, broad-browed and muscular. But Dakkar's mentor had been dark, whereas this man had long red hair tied in a ponytail and a long thick beard. He reminded Dakkar of a Viking warrior, with a thick leather belt and leather breeches. This Oginski wore the scorpion of Serqet on his chest, though.

'No doubt you are impressed by the way we control the insects below?' the man said. He lifted a silver whistle that hung on a chain round his neck. 'The whistle confuses them and then the perfume bomb pacifies them.'

'What are they?' Yunus growled. 'Surely such beasts never walked the face of this earth. They must be creatures of the Devil!'

'These creatures are called ant lions. They come from a world deep within the earth.' Oginski said, nodding at Dakkar. 'He knows of where I speak. Normally, such insects would be tiny but down there, in that strange land at the heart of the Earth, they grow to enormous size.'

'You should have left them down below,' Dakkar spat. 'What's going on? Who *are* you?'

'He's Marek Oginski,' Georgia said. 'Voychek is a master of disguise, remember? This guy's not hiding much.'

Marek grinned and gave a smile of approval. 'You are clever, young lady,' he said. 'It is true that I did go by that name before I was blessed by the sting of Serqet.' Again, all the men touched the tattoos on their chests. 'Now my mind is set on more spiritual matters.'

'Like making people into slaves and building an army in London?' Dakkar sneered. 'Doesn't sound very spiritual to me!'

Marek's smile faded and he narrowed his eyes. 'You can mock me if you wish, Prince Dakkar, but Serqet is the goddess who stings the unrighteous and brings them to judgement. Her venom is revenge. I have made it my holy quest to destroy you. You have the blood of my brothers on your hands. I have promised *your* blood to my goddess.'

'You're insane,' Dakkar murmured.

'Am I? You're the one so consumed with hatred and rage that you need to kill every last Oginski,' Marek said softly. 'I knew you would chase me here. I knew you couldn't resist hunting me down even in the middle of this vast, hostile desert. I know you better than you know yourself.'

'I know why I'm here,' Dakkar said.

'To clear your name after I made you look guilty for the murder of that buffoon of an Englishman?' Marek said. 'Ha! Once I distracted Blizzard by kidnapping those Cornish villagers and sending him on a diplomatic mission, I knew you wouldn't be able to resist the rather obvious trail of clues I left. I'm impressed that you got so close to me. It shows your thirst for Oginski blood is strong!'

'That's not true,' Georgia cut in. 'We came to stop you, not necessarily to kill . . .'

Marek snorted, ignoring her but still focusing on Dakkar. 'Is that what you tell yourself about my brothers?' He said. 'About Kazmer? Or Stefan? Borys or Tomasz? Or Franciszek?' Dakkar flinched at the name of his mentor but Marek pressed on. 'Oh yes, my prince, you were as responsible for Franciszek's death as Tomasz was! You killed ALL my brothers!'

'That's a lie!' Dakkar screamed, hurling himself forward. With his arms bound, he stumbled, falling headlong at Marek's feet.

'You are finished, Prince Dakkar,' Marek said, looking down at him with disdain. 'Defeated. And now I shall sacrifice you to my goddess!'

CHAPTER SEVENTEEN
SERQET

Bound and exhausted, Dakkar and his companions were jostled and pushed towards the fortress. Marek rode a camel at the head of the column of men. Georgia staggered alongside him, but every now and then she would look over her shoulder or strain to see the ridges of the dunes in the distance.

'What are you looking for?' Dakkar said, his patience breaking.

'Karim,' Georgia whispered. 'He was up on the dune when we fell into the pit. I think he's following us.'

'He did well to escape being captured,' Dakkar hissed back. 'Maybe he'll be able to rescue us.'

'Or go for help!' Georgia replied.

Dakkar wrestled with the ropes. 'We can't rely on that, though,' he said. 'If Karim did go for help, it wouldn't arrive for days, and if he attacks, he is only one man. And poor little Ibrahim is trapped in the *Nautilus* still.'

A tattooed guard swatted Dakkar with the flat of his sword. 'Stop talking!' the man snarled. 'Or you'll be dragged behind the master's camel.'

A rifle shot rang out across the sands and the man fell, blood gushing from his tattooed chest. The rest of the column dropped to the ground. Dakkar saw Marek expertly dismount and drag his camel down, hiding behind the cover of its body.

A second shot killed another man close to Dakkar. He died twitching on the sand where he lay.

'My prince!' Karim shouted from the dunes above them. 'Are you hurt?'

Dakkar could see him now. He lay a short distance away, sheltered by the crest of the dune.

'I am unharmed, Karim!' Dakkar shouted back.

'You can't hope to kill us all,' Marek called out. 'You are one; we are many. Men from the fort will overwhelm you before you escape.'

'Send your prisoners over and we'll see about that,' Karim said, sending another shot buzzing over Marek's head.

Karim ducked down, obviously reloading. Marek stood up and rummaged in his saddlebags, bringing out a glass globe full of red liquid. Marek looked over at Dakkar and grinned. 'I used blue oil last time,' he said. 'Watch the difference between the two.'

Dakkar's heart thumped. 'Karim, run!' he shouted, but Marek stood up and hurled the globe. It was a powerful throw and the glass ball sailed in an arc. Dakkar saw

Karim's puzzled face peer over the dune and heard the glass tinkle as the globe smashed close to him.

'What is this?' Karim said, his voice mocking Marek. 'You try to kill me with perfume?'

'Karim, get off the dune!' Dakkar yelled.

Marek still stood. Karim fired another shot but his aim failed. Dakkar saw a lock of Marek's red hair flutter to the ground but he remained unharmed.

'I'm not killing you with perfume,' Marek called. 'I'm just summoning something . . . hungry!' Sand began to stream down the sides of the dune. Karim stood up, staring at his feet as the ground beneath him shook. Dakkar threw himself forward but some of the guards had leapt to their feet and grabbed hold of him.

'Run, Karim!' he screamed.

Karim gave a final yell and then disappeared in a fountain of blood and sand. Then the dune fell still again. Tears stung Dakkar's eyes and he fell to his knees.

'The creatures here are controlled by a scent we have perfected,' Marek said. 'One oil calms them and makes them almost sleepy, the other drives them into a destructive feeding frenzy as your poor friend just found out. A loyal man, but he wasted his life for you, Prince Dakkar. As so many have before.'

They trudged in silence through the burning sand until the fortress came clearly into view. It was, as Dakkar had guessed, a walled square of mud brick. Guards patrolled the walls and looked down as the tall wooden gates, engraved with scorpions, swung open to let the column in.

As they stepped inside, Georgia gave a gasp. 'You wouldn't think we were in a desert at all,' she said. A round pool of clear water filled the centre of the stockade and palms hung over its edge. Vines crept over the buildings that nestled in the shadow of the high walls. Opposite them stood a building with a grand front. Carved scorpions scuttled all over the rows of columns and arched windows that stood either side of a huge door.

'Reminds me of St Paul's Cathedral,' Fletcher whispered.

'It is the Temple of Serqet,' Marek said, kissing his hand and touching his heart. 'Where we worship and sacrifice.'

'So you've turned your back on Cryptos then?' Dakkar said, hoping to goad Marek.

Marek gave a chilling smile and lowered his voice. 'Let's just say the aims of Cryptos and the Vengeance of Serqet complement each other nicely,' he said. 'The righteous shall be saved and the unworthy shall perish at the hands of Cryptos. My brothers ruled their men by fear. These guards would die for their goddess' – Marek's smile grew and he pointed to himself – 'or their high priest.'

'Dakkar, look,' Georgia hissed, and nodded to where men strode along the base of the walls with globes of perfume. Every now and then they stopped and chanted, sprinkling some of the blue oil into the sand.

'Interesting,' Dakkar muttered, narrowing his eyes.

The cool of the huge hall they were pushed into enveloped them and, for a moment, Dakkar was blind in the darkness of the place. Slowly his eyes grew accustomed to the gloom lit by a few guttering torches.

'It *is* like a cathedral,' Fletcher said again. Dakkar couldn't disagree. Tall pillars lined a central aisle that led to the back of the hall. Here, at the top of raised steps, a figure sat on a throne. A mist of incense shrouded the figure and filled Dakkar's mouth and nose. He swallowed, fighting the urge to spit.

Strange, discordant hand bells chimed from behind the pillars at their side and Dakkar became aware of men kneeling. They began chanting rhythmically.

Suddenly Dakkar was pushed to his knees at the bottom step. A woman sat on the throne, staring down at him with heavy-lidded green eyes. She wore black silken robes that shimmered blue and purple like the shell of a scorpion. Her long black hair flowed over her shoulder and on her head sat a crown fashioned into the shape of a scorpion ready to strike. Dakkar couldn't judge her age; she was older than him. But she was so beautiful!

The bells rang again, randomly, and the chanting grew. Dakkar could see two scorpion acolytes swinging incense burners now, thickening the smoke. Marek walked over to an altar encrusted with carved scorpions and picked up an ornate bottle; he then poured the contents of the bottle into a golden cup.

'The venom of Serqet!' Marek bellowed, raising the cup.

'Vengeance be hers,' murmured the congregation. Marek stepped forward and placed the cup to the woman's lips. For a second, panic flashed in her green eyes, then the liquid touched her lips and they became vacant and serene. Her head slumped forward for a moment, then she raised it up and stared at Dakkar.

'Who are these strangers?' she said, her voice distant.

'Intruders, oh holy Serqet,' Marek said as he knelt before her. 'We bring them before you to ask: do we spare them or do we sacrifice?'

Serqet looked vacantly at Marek as if she were somewhere else. 'Sacrifice,' she repeated. Her rouged lips didn't close completely after she had spoken.

'Your holiness . . . Serqet,' Dakkar began but an acolyte pushed his head down.

'How dare you speak to the goddess,' he spat.

There was a moment's pause and Serqet stared over their heads. 'Speak to the goddess,' she sighed.

The acolyte looked confused and glanced at Marek, who glowered at him.

'Serqet, we mean no harm,' Dakkar began, staying on his knees. 'We came because some of your servants were taking slaves from England and . . .'

Serqet frowned. 'England.' She breathed the word rather than spoke it and a single tear trickled down her cheek.

'Enough!' Marek barked. 'Oh mighty Serqet, shall we make a sacrifice?'

Serqet blinked and frowned. 'A sacrifice,' she repeated.

'It is done!' Marek said, standing and turning to the acolytes who knelt around the steps. 'A sacrifice! Prepare a sacrifice!'

Dakkar, Georgia, Fletcher and Yunus were dragged to their feet by the acolytes and bundled to a small cell at the side of the temple. A single barred window at the top of the wall let a shaft of daylight in.

'Serqet is tired!' Marek said. Dakkar noticed his hand gripping the goddess's upper arm in a most irreverent manner.

Serqet turned her head slowly back to Dakkar and stared at him. 'England,' he heard her say before he was pushed into the cell. The door slammed shut. Outside more bells began to ring and the chanting grew more frantic.

'Let us out, you heathen dogs!' Yunus said, pounding a fist on the door.

'Save your strength,' Dakkar replied. 'I think we're going to need it.'

CHAPTER EIGHTEEN
MAREK'S PLAN

Time in the dark, dusty cell lost its meaning. The chanting and clashing of bells and the heavy incense made Dakkar drowsy. He shook himself. The others languished on the small pallet bed or sat on the floor.

The grille in the door slid open and Marek peered through. 'Are you comfortable, princeling?' he sneered.

'What are you up to, Marek?' Dakkar growled. 'Why all the façade of the scorpion cult? All this nonsense isn't Cryptos's style.'

'He's right. Only last year you blew up Mount Tambora in the Far East,' Fletcher added. 'Didn't Blizzard say so, Dakkar? Thousands were killed and that's why we're having all this bad weather now.'

'All that famine and people getting hungry,' Georgia said. 'An ideal time for you to take control. So why are you holed up in the middle of the desert?'

'Because that is only part of the plan,' Marek snarled. 'And it wasn't me who blew up Mount Tambora.'

'Then it must have been Voychek,' Dakkar said, striding towards the door.

Marek laughed. 'You really don't know what's going on, do you? Rome wasn't built in a day, as the old saying goes, and nor will Cryptos's empire be built overnight.'

'So you build an army in London,' Georgia said. 'Take over there. Is that the start of it?'

Marek's shoulders were shaking. 'You are a clever girl,' he said through his laughter. 'But the rabble that is growing in London is just a distraction.' He stopped laughing and became deadly serious. 'Already the *Serqet*, sailing under Dutch colours, leaves Algiers, heading for London. Its hold is full of canisters and explosives. Each canister is full of a deadly poison gas manufactured from the venom of our giant scorpions. The gas paralyses and eventually kills any living thing. It is a slow, painful death.'

'I don't understand . . .' Dakkar began.

'My ragged army in London will storm the government buildings, drawing the full attention of the military,' Marek said, striding back to the throne. 'At the same time, the *Serqet* will enter the Thames. She will explode and the gas will strip London bare of its inhabitants. With no effective government, Britain will be ripe for the plucking and Cryptos will make the harvest. We will send more ships to Paris and Rome, to New York and Washington. We will drop the gas from the air. Cryptos will rule this world.'

'Your men might not share your ambitions,' Dakkar said.

Marek snorted. 'Have you seen them? They are devoted to Serqet and this woman has become Serqet in human form. I could have ruled by fear like my brothers, Stefan and Kazmer. This way is far more effective. My men would throw themselves to their deaths for her without a second's hesitation. I control her. Besides,' he said darkly, 'she has another ability. One which might prove useful in the future.'

'What other ability?' Dakkar said, lacing his voice with sarcasm. 'Can she perform magic?'

Marek snorted. 'Let's just say she can see through the most ingenious disguises,' he said, 'and there might be a time when I need that skill. But enough of her. I want you to appreciate, Prince Dakkar, how sweet your sacrifice to Serqet will be for me. In some ways, I'm impressed. My brother Kazmer once identified you as a worthy successor and future leader of Cryptos but you turned out to be even more ruthless than he could have imagined . . .'

'I'm not ruthless . . .'

Marek dismissed Dakkar's protest with a wave of his hand. 'You were Franciszek Oginski's attack dog. A little yapping terrier, with a ferocious bite,' he said. 'I'd admire that if you hadn't killed so many of my family.'

'Your family chose to attack me,' Dakkar said coldly. 'Your family formed an organisation determined to spread misery and destruction, and why? To seek some kind of revenge over the death of one girl?'

'Celina was truly beautiful,' Marek said, his voice becoming distant, as if he were reliving that tragic part of his life. 'Not just beautiful to look upon but she was kind and gentle. You would have fallen for her if you'd met her, Dakkar.'

'Would she approve of what you are now?' Dakkar said sullenly.

Marek ignored him. 'But when the Tsar's men invaded our homeland, burning and destroying everything and everyone in their path, her kindness counted for nothing.'

'So you became as bad as the men who killed her?' Georgia began.

Marek's face flushed red. 'We made them pay!'

'Killing so many innocents in the process,' Dakkar added.

'Ha! Innocence?' Marek said. 'Nobody can be trusted. I'm sure even the gentle Celina would have taken a blade to the throat of the soldiers who killed her parents if she'd had the chance.' Marek paused for a moment, reflecting on the past. 'All I'm doing is setting the world to rights again. All men are greedy; all men desire power. It is natural to them. We will crush that greed and bring peace to the world. There will be no more war, no more petty border squabbles. Cryptos will reign supreme and people will flourish.'

'You're mad,' Dakkar said. 'How will your rule be any different to a hundred kings or queens in years gone by?'

Marek glared back at him. 'Because we will wield absolute power. Any who oppose us will perish. Whole cities, whole nations if necessary.'

'That's horrible,' Georgia said, her voice quiet.

'No more horrible than what has happened in the past.' Marek sounded sad. 'We have a chance to change the world. We can wipe out these governments who think they know best. My brothers knew this and I will finish our mission in their name.'

'You all turned against the world, caused so much misery and pain, because one girl was killed?' Dakkar said, holding Marek's gaze until the man looked away.

'You aren't the person to lecture me, Prince Dakkar,' Marek said. 'How many men died when you brought down my brothers' flying fortress? How many died when you blew up my brother Stefan's tower in the underworld? How many when you destroyed Kazmer's volcanic home?'

'They brought that on themselves,' Dakkar said.

Marek shrugged. 'And that's enough?' he said. 'Then the nations of the world have brought this judgement on themselves too. And I will avenge my brothers. Prepare yourself, Prince Dakkar. The sacrifice ritual will be finished within the hour. Your death is near.'

CHAPTER NINETEEN
SACRIFICE

The chanting and ringing of bells grew louder and drums joined the general cacophony. Dakkar paced from the window to the door, alternately jumping up to glimpse the outside world and kicking the hard wood that blocked their way to freedom. They had managed between them to loosen and untie the ropes that bound them but they were still trapped.

'If that woman is a goddess,' Georgia said, 'then I'm George Washington's grandmother!'

'What did you expect?' Dakkar replied. He paused for a moment. 'Did you see her face when I mentioned England?'

'She is a European,' Yunus said, nodding at Fletcher. 'Like your friends.'

'I'm an American, I'll have you know,' Georgia cut in without missing a beat. 'But yeah, she was English, I reckon.'

'She looked drugged. I reckon old Marek slips something into that cup he gives her,' Fletcher said. 'I remember in old Ma Crampley's a chap slipped something into Flinty Wiltshire's drink. He fell down like a skittle!'

'Could you say that in English?' Georgia asked. 'I got the drugged bit but . . .'

'Never mind that,' Dakkar snapped. 'I think you're right, Fletcher. I think she is here against her will just like us. Maybe we can use that to our advantage.'

A scrabbling sound followed by a hollow bump came from the window and a head blotted out the column of sunlight that shone through. At first they couldn't make out who it was but then Dakkar saw a pair of brown eyes and a smudged face.

'Ibrahim!' Dakkar gasped. 'They haven't found you?'

'Forgive me, your highness, but when those terrible creatures attacked,' Ibrahim whispered rapidly, 'I hid. I didn't know what to do. So now I have crept out and have come to save you. You will be glad I came along!'

'I hope so, Ibrahim,' Dakkar said. 'But how did you get into the fortress?'

'I was about to sneak out and follow you but some men began to throw ropes over your ship. They dragged it inside the fortress. And here I am!'

Dakkar shook his head in wonder at the boy. 'So the *Nautilus* is just outside. That's a stroke of luck. Can you move around the fortress easily?'

'Yes, your princeliness,' Ibrahim said in wonder. 'I am small. Nobody notices Ibrahim. Everyone seems to have gone into this temple. They are all shouting and banging drums. It is giving me a headache.'

'We can hear that for ourselves, boy,' Yunus said, following the conversation.

'Try to find some weapons; guns or powder would be best but anything you can,' Dakkar said, ignoring Yunus.

'I have already done that.' Ibrahim grinned, pushing two pistols through the bars of the window. 'They are loaded so be careful. Here is some more powder and shot.'

'Good lad,' Dakkar said, stuffing the pistol into the back of his belt. 'Where did you get these?' He passed the other pistol to Georgia.

'Same place as I found these,' Ibrahim said, passing through another two. 'There is a storeroom on the other side of the fort. It is full of weapons and oil.' Ibrahim frowned as if puzzled by the last item. 'Lots of tall jars of oil, some red and some blue.' He shrugged. 'They smell funny. I don't know what they are.'

'I think I do,' Dakkar said. 'Ibrahim, I want you to go back to the storeroom. Is it safe to do that?'

'Not safe, your highness, but I can do it easily,' Ibrahim said with a grin.

'Good, then go back there and smash all the red jars,' Dakkar said. 'But don't get any of the oil on yourself – that is very important. Then hurry back to this side of the fortress and wait for us.'

'Consider it done, my prince,' Ibrahim said and vanished from sight.

'And get some more powder if you can!' Dakkar said, but he didn't know if the boy had heard him.

'Dax, what is going on?' Georgia said, hands on her hips. The conversation had been in Turkish and she and Fletcher hadn't understood a word.

'Total chaos, I hope.' Dakkar grinned. He looked at the pistols they held. 'We're still too poorly armed to defeat all of them. Surprise must be our ally.' He picked up the ropes that had bound their hands and, once the others had concealed their weapons under shirts and robes, tied them loosely around the others' wrists. 'Wait for my signal before you use the guns. If we can get close to Serqet, we may be able to hold her hostage.'

Time passed, each minute seeming like an hour, until finally the lock rattled and two acolytes stood at the door. Their eyes were wide and they trembled slightly with anticipation of the sacrifice.

'Come with us,' one of them said. 'Serqet is rested. The ritual is almost complete. It is time for sacrifice.'

Dakkar led the others out into the hall. The chanting was rhythmic and hypnotic; bells rang and symbols clashed and the incense nearly choked him. Acolytes filled the temple but Dakkar noticed that the central aisle was kept clear. They were led up the aisle to the steps where Marek stood glowering at them. Serqet sat on her throne, her eyes drowsy, her head almost lolling on her shoulder.

Dakkar's guard pushed him to his knees but Dakkar stood up again. 'Your "goddess" looks a tad fatigued,' he sneered.

Marek just nodded to the guard, who kicked Dakkar's legs from under him. Dakkar fell painfully, groaning.

'You should show more respect, princeling,' Marek growled. 'You have but a few moments to live. It is time for the sacrifice!' The acolytes roared their approval, deafening Dakkar.

Marek pulled a lever. The steps beneath Dakkar trembled and he turned to see the floor of the central aisle open to reveal a pit with a seething black floor. At first Dakkar thought it was some kind of liquid, but then he realised that the pit was full of scorpions climbing over each other in a clicking, seething mass of shining black.

'Soon you shall be one with Serqet in the Pit of Death,' Marek said, laughing.

'You're mad,' Dakkar said, creeping back up the steps away from the edge of the newly opened pit. The chanting grew louder.

Marek strode towards Dakkar but Yunus broke his loosely tied ropes and pulled the pistol from his boot. The gun went off and Dakkar saw a spray of blood from Marek's shoulder but the big man barely seemed to notice it. He turned on Yunus and picked him up in one motion.

'Yunus!' Dakkar cried, jumping up, but Marek hurled the poor guard down into the pit.

Yunus screamed as he plunged into the writhing mass of scorpions, twisting and turning as they stung him countless times. But then the pile of creatures surged up and a huge pair of claws bust through the smaller scorpions. Two red eyes and an armoured body followed, then long, stick-like legs and a powerful tail. The claws fastened on Yunus's twitching body and then tore him apart.

The crowd in the temple roared Serqet's name and even Marek seemed hypnotised by the sight.

Trying not to think of what he'd just seen, Dakkar broke free, leaping past Marek, pulling his pistol out from its hiding place and pointing it at Serqet. He circled round behind the throne, keeping the gun pointed at her temple.

'Nobody move or we'll see just how immortal this goddess really is!' Dakkar snarled.

The acolytes fell silent and stared in horror at Dakkar.

Georgia and Fletcher had broken free too and levelled their guns on Marek.

'You think you can escape?' Marek said. 'The fortress is surrounded by my guardian beetles. You'll never get away.'

As if in reply to Marek's statement, the whole temple shook.

'I think your beetles have come in to say hello,' Dakkar said with a grin.

CHAPTER TWENTY
POISON PRIEST

Marek looked in horror and disbelief. 'What have you done?' he said. The whole temple trembled.

'Your ant lions aren't as easy to control as you'd have us believe,' Dakkar said. 'That's why you have your acolytes sprinkling the blue perfume that pacifies them all around the edge of the fortress. It keeps you safe. I just arranged to have the other oil, the red one that calls them to lunch, spilt all over the storeroom . . .'

'You fool.' Marek took a step forward. The temple shivered again and the brown, bulbous head of an ant lion burst through the back wall, its pincer mouth gripping an acolyte around his waist. Men screamed and ran outside. Two pillars fell into the pit, forming a ramp up into the temple, and the huge scorpion began to crawl out.

'Don't move, Marek,' Dakkar snapped and Georgia and Fletcher twitched their pistols. Dakkar turned to

Serqet, who still sat staring into space, oblivious to the crashing masonry and screaming men. 'Can you hear me?' he said, putting his lips close to her ear. She nodded slowly. 'We're getting away. Going back to England,' Dakkar said. 'Will you come?'

She turned her head and gave him a sleepy grin. 'England,' she said, her voice slurred.

'You're not going anywhere,' Marek snarled, taking a step forward. 'I spent years building this cult of unquestioning acolytes. They won't let you just take their goddess away!' Lumps of rock and mud brick were thudding from the ceiling now and dust replaced the incense. A huge chunk of stone crashed down between Georgia and Fletcher, forcing them to leap aside. Fletcher's pistol misfired and Georgia tumbled down the steps, almost falling into the pit. Marek saw his chance.

The huge man sprang forward, swatting Dakkar's pistol aside and grabbing his arm. Suddenly Dakkar found himself pinned to the floor with Marek's fingers around his throat.

Dakkar seized the man's wrist and hand, trying to break his grip, but Marek had the strength of madness. Even punching him repeatedly in the side of the head just made him grin more manically.

'You're going to die, Prince Dakkar,' he spat, bringing his face close to Dakkar's. 'And then your friends will follow.'

'You'll never succeed now,' Dakkar gasped, his voice hoarse.

'You think I need all this?' Marek said, tightening his grip. 'Foolish boy. My ship, the *Serqet*, is ploughing the sea as we speak, taking its deadly cargo to England!'

Dakkar's head felt like it was about to explode. His heart pounded. Something moved in the corner of his blurring vision and his eyes widened.

The giant scorpion had clambered out of the pit and up the steps. But Marek was too intent on throttling Dakkar to notice. Dakkar thrashed, desperate to get away, but Marek held on.

Dakkar tried to speak but Marek's grip was too tight. Twisting and wriggling, Dakkar managed to get his feet squarely against Marek's chest. The temple was fading from Dakkar's sight as he gave one final push with his legs. He could taste blood in his mouth as he strained every muscle, trying to force Marek off. Slowly, Marek's hold weakened slightly, letting breath into Dakkar's lungs. Marek's sweaty hands trembled as he tried to regain his grip. Then the big man stumbled backward, propelled by Dakkar's kick.

For a second, Marek stood at the top of the steps, a look of astonishment on his face as the huge black pincers closed round his waist from behind. Then the scorpion's tail lashed down, driving its poisoned spike through Marek's back and shoulder.

Marek's eyes bulged and a trickle of blood oozed from the corner of his mouth. He stared at Dakkar.

'You think you've won,' Marek gasped. 'You'll never win, Prince Dakkar. My ship has already left for London.

And my brother . . . will . . .' – Marek's eyes glazed over and he fixed his eyes on Serqet – '. . . have the last . . .' he said, and began to laugh.

A swift crunch ended Marek's laughter as the scorpion closed its pincers, cutting the big man in half. Dakkar turned his head and saw Serqet smiling serenely at the gory mess. Dakkar's stomach lurched. The scorpion was climbing over the remains of Marek towards them.

Aching in every limb, his breath rasping from his crushed throat, Dakkar inched back towards the goddess, searching for his pistol. Beyond the scorpion, the temple was still in chaos. The huge ant lion had been joined by another, and acolytes tried to subdue them with clubs and spears. More and more bodies lay among the debris and an incense burner had overturned, spreading flames across the temple. Behind Dakkar, the goddess sat staring into the distance as if nothing was happening.

A bullet buzzed across the dais they stood on and smacked into the eye of the scorpion. It reared up, spreading its claws wide.

'Grab a weapon, Dax!' Georgia shouted, hastily reloading. 'There.' She pointed to a body not far from Dakkar. Fletcher appeared from behind a chunk of fallen roof and snatched up a sword, throwing it to Dakkar.

The scorpion crashed down in front of Dakkar, its claws slicing through the air inches from his face. Still dizzy, Dakkar staggered back towards Serqet, who still watched as if she were in a dream.

Another bullet smacked into the scorpion's thick shell

and Dakkar swung his sword down. It clanged uselessly off the creature's claw. Fletcher fired, sending a chunk of the creature's carapace spinning off into the pit. The scorpion scuttled round to face him, raising its claws.

'Don't let it get you,' Dakkar shouted, glancing sidelong at the torn body of Marek that lay on the bloodsoaked steps. The scorpion's tail curled up behind its body, ready to strike. But Fletcher was too slow; the scorpion leapt forward and gripped him by the thigh. The tail started on its journey down.

Without thinking, Dakkar swung his sword, gripping it with both hands, his eyes focused on one of the joints in the tail. *Surely there must be a weakness there.*

Time slowed. Dakkar could see the dull light of fires that had sprung up around the temple glinting on the flat of his sword. He could see the sheen of purple and blue on the scorpion's tail. Then the blade bit into the tail, sending splinters of armour cascading off in all directions. But the speed of the tail's swing helped Dakkar's blow and he grinned as the sharp edge cut through the tail, sending the poisoned tip spinning into the darkness.

Fletcher kicked into the scorpion's bloody face, his heel finding another eye. The creature let go and he managed to drag himself away, while Dakkar circled round in front of it. But at that moment an acolyte, wild-eyed and brandishing a sword, leapt between them, as if protecting the scorpion. He brought his sword down.

Dakkar parried the blow. 'Get out of the way, you fool, it'll . . .' But his words were drowned by the acolyte's screams as the scorpion's pincers clamped on to the man's waist. The acolyte kicked and dropped his sword, struggling to get free. A huge rumbling shook the temple and a pile of masonry buried both acolyte and scorpion.

Dakkar darted forward and grabbed the goddess from her throne. She blinked at him as he pulled her to her feet. 'Quickly,' he shouted to Georgia and Fletcher. 'We have to get out. This whole place is about to collapse.'

Dragging the goddess behind them, they ran, dodging falling masonry that smashed on to the tiled floor. One or two acolytes lunged at them but Dakkar punched out with his sword hand, giving them the hilt in their faces.

Dust and smoke filled the room now, making them cough and splutter as they ran. Serqet stumbled along behind Dakkar, the same fixed smile on her face. A rectangle of light shone through the fog in the temple, showing them the way out.

'This way,' Dakkar said, dragging the goddess by the hand. The light vanished, blotted out by a huge round shape. Dakkar gasped. An ant lion loomed over them in the doorway. Dakkar could see his face reflected a thousand times in the bulbous compound eyes.

'Over here,' Georgia yelled, ducking to the side of the temple. A column had fallen against its neighbour and wooden beams from above had wedged against them, forming a lopsided shelter against the debris that clattered down from above.

The ant lion gave a hiss and stepped forward.

'Dakkar, look out!' Fletcher cried, pulling him and Serqet into the uncertain safety of the fallen column. Directly behind him, a pair of claws reared over his head as the scorpion burst out of the debris that had covered it.

Glancing down, Dakkar saw a body with a red phial of oil on its belt. Grimacing at the blood that stained the white robes of the body, Dakkar pulled the bottle of oil free and hurled it at the scorpion, watching with grim satisfaction as it smashed over the creature's back. The ant lion waved its antennae and stormed towards the scorpion. The scorpion's tail stabbed uselessly at the ant lion as the two locked pincers.

'Out now, while we can,' Dakkar yelled above the rumbling that filled the temple. 'We must get to the *Nautilus* and stop the *Serqet* from reaching London!'

They ran towards the clear doorway, jumping back as the scorpion cut one of the ant lion's legs off. The insect hissed and fixed its huge pincers on to the claws of the scorpion.

Daylight blinded them as they staggered out of the gloom and chaos of the temple. Dakkar looked back and caught a last glimpse of the scorpion and the ant lion locked together. Then what was left of the roof and walls collapsed in, burying the two monsters.

Masonry and beams crashed down, bouncing out into the courtyard of the fortress. Dakkar and the others had to throw themselves to the ground to avoid being hit by flying debris.

'We've got to find Ibrahim!' Dakkar yelled above the chaos.

More ant lions scuttled around the fortress. Some had been killed by the acolytes, but many of the men lay dead on the sand or had vanished down new holes dug by the giant insects.

A cry went up and a small group of acolytes ran towards them, shouting, 'Serqet! Save the goddess!' Those who weren't trying to subdue the ant lions joined the group.

'We need to get out of here, now,' Georgia said, scanning the courtyard. 'I thought Ibrahim said they had brought the *Nautilus* inside the fortress.'

'He did,' Dakkar replied. But there was no sign of their ship or of Ibrahim. Both had vanished.

CHAPTER TWENTY-ONE
FIRE FROM ABOVE

The acolytes waved clubs and swords as they ran towards Dakkar and Serqet. Georgia started loading her pistol again.

'We can't stop them all,' Dakkar said. 'There must be at least eighteen of them.'

'Eighteen,' Serqet murmured, smiling at the charging mob.

Dakkar had an idea. He turned to Serqet and shook her gently. 'Serqet, listen,' he said. 'Order those men to lay down their arms!'

Serqet blinked her heavily lidded eyes. 'England,' she said, smiling. 'Arms.'

'It's no good,' Fletcher said, searching around for somewhere to run to. The oasis lay at the heart of the fortress and various buildings lined the inside of the walls but there was nowhere obvious to hide. 'Dunno where to go,' he said, his face long. 'No alleys to hide in here.'

The men were close now. Dakkar could see their scorpion tattoos and angry faces. He lifted his sword. 'Please, tell them to stand still.'

'Stand still,' Serqet whispered in a distant voice that her acolytes would never hear.

The men ignored her, intent on rescue. Dakkar's heart pounded. Options were running out fast.

An explosion erupted in the middle of the group, throwing sand high into the air and sending men flying over the heads of others. Another followed, scattering the crowd of acolytes.

Dakkar looked up and saw the *Nautilus* describing a tight circle above them. Ibrahim stood on the front deck, holding on to a handle with one hand and gripping a sea arrow in the other. He grinned down, looking for his next target, and threw one at an ant lion that scuttled past with an acolyte screaming in its jaws. The insect's huge body disintegrated into a disgusting black puddle.

'Ibrahim!' Dakkar yelled. 'What are you doing up there? Bring the ship down so we can get on board!'

Ibrahim's face fell. 'I can't, master!' he said. 'After the monsters broke in through the walls, I hid in the ship. But when the temple collapsed, I pushed some levers and ended up floating round and round!'

'You're lucky you didn't just go sailing up into the sun!' Dakkar shouted, looking sternly at him.

The acolytes had regrouped but Ibrahim hurled another sea arrow down at them, sending them scurrying for cover.

'Look!' Georgia said, pointing to a rope that trailed

along the sand from the stern of the *Nautilus* as it drifted in its tight circle. 'If one of us can climb that rope, then he can bring the *Nautilus* down and we can all get aboard.'

'He?' Dakkar flashed a brief grin at Georgia. 'If you don't like heights, it's all right to say so,' he said, hurrying towards the rope.

'I never said I . . .' Georgia stuttered, but Dakkar had already grabbed the rope and begun pulling himself up.

The rope twisted as Dakkar shinned up it. His arms ached and his head still pounded from Marek's throttling. He spun as he climbed, the ground getting further away with each lurch and pull.

Five acolytes remained of the group below; others had been knocked out by the explosions or thrown across the courtyard and were now fighting off ant lions. They hurried towards Fletcher, Georgia and Serqet.

A bullet whizzed past Dakkar, making him cling to the rope and hunch up. He scanned around wildly, searching for the marksman.

'Georgia!' he yelled. 'Can you occupy the rifleman on the wall? One more shot like that and he'll have my range. I'll be a sitting duck!'

The rifleman stood on the wall of the fortress, and was hurriedly reloading. Dakkar saw Georgia fire her pistol up at the walls, then turned his attention back to climbing. *We've got to get away from here and stop the* Serqet *delivering the deadly gas*, he thought.

The huge hull of the *Nautilus* blotted out the sun and Dakkar was able to see the polished planks and brass rivets that held it all together. Beneath him, he could see the ship's vast shadow cast on the distant ground. On the far side of the compound, a fire had taken hold and was raging through the buildings there. Dakkar saw men desperately ferrying water from the oasis, dodging ant lions to douse the flames. But now wasn't the time to be looking around, especially as the five acolytes grabbed the end of the rope.

Dakkar gripped on tight as the rope began to dance. The acolytes were swinging it as hard as they could, hoping to shake Dakkar off. The rope bit into his hands and his head banged on the hull of the ship.

He glanced down and saw the ground and the knot of acolytes swaying back and forth. A pistol cracked and Dakkar saw Fletcher charging forward with a sword in his hand. One of the acolytes had fallen to his pistol but four remained. Georgia looked to be reloading while Serqet stood, staring around, in a daze.

The rope had stopped its wild swinging now and Dakkar hurried up, reaching the side of the hull and bracing his aching legs against it. Now he could 'walk' himself up the side of the ship while leaning out and holding on to the rope. He peered below. Fletcher had knocked down another of the acolytes but there were still three of them. Georgia's pistol cracked and Dakkar saw a puff of smoke. Another acolyte fell to the floor but the two now had hold of Fletcher.

Ibrahim grabbed Dakkar's hand and helped him up on the deck. 'I can't throw any more bombs,' he said, pointing at Fletcher, who was backing away from the two men. 'Your English servant is too close.'

'Come on, let's land the *Nautilus* and even the odds a little,' Dakkar said, clambering up the tower ladder.

Once inside, Dakkar settled himself into the captain's seat and deflated the balloons slowly. As he glanced around the courtyard, he noticed that fewer ant lions scurried around, having dragged prey down into the earth. More acolytes were hurrying towards them as they descended.

'Ibrahim,' Dakkar said. 'Down in the lower cabin where I presume you hid, there are spare rifles and powder. Bring up as many as you can.'

'Yes, your highness!' Ibrahim said, hurrying down into the main body of the ship. Fletcher and his two pursuers were no longer under the ship. Dakkar began cranking the friction-wheel handle that poked out of the wall of the cabin. This generated an electric charge that had proved very effective in water, but he wondered how good it would be on dry land.

Ibrahim appeared with three rifles hugged to his chest. One almost slid back down the ladder. He dumped them next to Dakkar's seat and hurried back for powder and shot.

When he reappeared, he dumped the sack of powder on the floor and frowned at the wheel. 'What does that do, your greatness?'

'You'll see,' Dakkar said. 'Do you know how to load a rifle?'

Ibrahim nodded. 'My father showed me before he died.' His face darkened. 'It will be a pleasure to shoot these monsters!'

The *Nautilus* bumped gently to the ground. Dakkar looked through the window while loading the last gun. Four men had climbed on to the deck and were walking cautiously up to the window.

'Ibrahim,' Dakkar said. The boy came to the window, scowling. Dakkar pointed at the red button under the friction wheel. 'Press that,' he said.

Ibrahim stabbed his thumb against the red button and laughed as the acolytes outside danced and squirmed, their arms outstretched and their hair standing on end. The charge subsided and the men fell from the deck, unconscious.

'Still works on dry land then.' Dakkar grinned. He scrambled up the tower with a rifle in his hand and climbed out on to its top.

Fletcher had found a rifle and was parrying sword blows, using it like a staff, while Georgia had somehow managed to wrestle her opponent's club off him and had just knocked him out with it.

Dakkar leaned his rifle on the edge of the tower rail and took aim. His shot winged the acolyte fighting with Fletcher. The man gripped his side and fell to his knees. Fletcher pushed him over and, grabbing Serqet's hand, ran across the courtyard towards the *Nautilus*. Another acolyte leapt at Georgia from the walls. Dakkar picked up the next rifle and shot him in the leg before the man could land. He hit the ground hard with a scream. Georgia sprinted past Fletcher and Serqet and clambered on to the *Nautilus*.

Fletcher was near now, but Serqet couldn't run; she staggered and stumbled, dragged along rather than propelling herself.

More men were appearing from the ruins and from some of the outhouses that still stood. These, Dakkar thought, were the wilier ones, the ones who had hidden away safely when all the trouble began. Slowly they emerged, guns and swords in hand, staring at their goddess, who was being stolen away.

Dakkar could hear Fletcher pleading with Serqet down below. 'Please, miss, climb the ladder. That's it, one rung at a time. Yes, one rung at a time.'

The acolytes were running across the courtyard. If they got to Fletcher and Serqet, they wouldn't stand a chance. Snatching the third rifle, Dakkar climbed down on to the deck. Serqet was halfway up the ladder but she wasn't moving fast enough. Fletcher hung behind her at the bottom, glancing over his shoulder as the acolytes charged towards them. In a few seconds he would be overrun.

CHAPTER TWENTY-TWO
PURSUIT THROUGH THE CLOUDS

Dakkar raised his rifle and fired, sending one acolyte to the floor, clutching his thigh. Fletcher grinned up gratefully then climbed up the ladder behind Serqet. Dakkar ran to the window at the base of the tower. Ibrahim stared out at him. Dakkar pointed to the lever at Ibrahim's foot.

'Pull that,' he shouted. Ibrahim frowned and reached for the friction wheel, looking hopeful. 'No! By your feet! That one!'

Ibrahim nodded and pulled the lever. The balloons hissed and swelled, making the ropes taut and slowly lifting the *Nautilus* up a little. Dakkar ran back to the deck and peered over the side.

'Fletcher, are you all right?' he called.

'I will be when I've dealt with this feller!' An acolyte had climbed on to the first rung of the ladder and Fletcher was stamping on the man's hands. But the acolyte looked wild-eyed and heedless of the pain.

Another gunshot cracked and the acolyte fell from the ladder. The *Nautilus* rose higher and the acolytes on the ground yelled with frustration. Georgia grinned over at Dakkar, then climbed down from the deck to help Serqet on board.

The craft jerked, sending Dakkar stumbling. He glimpsed Georgia grabbing hold of Serqet just in time to stop her falling from the ladder. The goddess had the same dreamy look on her face, as if none of this was happening. But the mob of angry acolytes had firm hold of the rope that Dakkar had climbed up and, gradually, the *Nautilus* sank towards the ground again.

Fletcher's face appeared over the deck but he looked grim. 'They're pulling us down!' he yelled.

'Use another bomb!' Ibrahim shouted from the tower, but Dakkar shook his head.

'We're too close to them now. It would rip open the hull,' he called back.

'What about the friction wheel?' Georgia said.

'We'd have to go inside and it doesn't work on anyone not actually standing on the boat,' Dakkar said, watching with growing panic as the ship neared the ground.

The acolytes' angry faces grew nearer as they heaved on the rope ladder. An explosion of sand and rock erupted beneath them and they were drifting up again. Down below, men screamed, and Dakkar realised that an ant lion had opened up a hole directly where the group of men had been standing. The insect's fierce pincers snapped at arms and legs and the injured men fell into the darkness of the chasm that yawned beneath them.

Dakkar turned away, sickened by the carnage below. A welcome cool breeze blew across the deck. He stood staring into the blue sky as the yells of the acolytes, the crackle of the flaming fortress and the smell of smoke became distant. Georgia stood at his shoulder.

'I've put the "goddess" in a guest cabin,' she said. 'She's sleeping.'

'Good,' Dakkar said, his voice flat.

'None of that was your fault, you know,' she said, looking down at the plumes of smoke drifting up from the distant fortress. 'Marek would have killed us all. He brought it on himself and the others down there.'

Dakkar turned to her. 'I know,' he said. 'But wherever we go there's destruction and death. I sometimes think I might be cursed.'

The engines began to hum, telling Dakkar that Fletcher had set a course.

'If we don't stop that ship full of gas then all of this destruction will have been pointless and many thousands of innocent people will perish,' Georgia said. A smudge of dirt stood out on her pale cheek.

'But we can never catch that ship in time,' Dakkar said, sitting down on the deck. 'It'll be out of the Mediterranean by now.'

'We're flying, stupid!' Georgia smiled. 'We can take the country lanes!'

'Country lanes?' Dakkar said. 'What are you on about?'

'We can fly across land,' Georgia said. 'In a straight line. We don't have to sail around Spain!'

Dakkar slapped his hand to his head. 'Of course!' he said. 'I wasn't thinking.' He leapt to his feet. 'Come on then,' he said. 'Let's go and catch that ship.'

Ibrahim stood with his arms folded and his bottom lip sticking out. He scowled up at Dakkar. 'I'm staying with you, your highness!' he growled.

'No, Ibrahim, it's too dangerous,' Dakkar said. 'We will drop you off outside the city and then carry on.'

'Too dangerous, my lord?' Ibrahim said, raising his eyebrows. 'Who rescued you from those scorpion men? It was I! I laugh in the face of danger. Nothing frightens me!'

'What did he say?' Georgia asked. Ibrahim stared at her wide-eyed.

'Except for her,' Ibrahim said in Turkish. 'She frightens me.'

'You ended up on this part of the mission by accident, pure and simple,' Dakkar said sternly. 'If you hadn't stowed away, you wouldn't have been in danger at all! No, I can't put you at risk.'

'He wants to stay?' Georgia said, raising one eyebrow at Ibrahim and making him flinch.

'Yes, but he's too young,' Dakkar said. 'He'll slow us down.'

Georgia pulled a face. 'He stole the weapons for us back at the fortress,' she said. 'I'd say he pulled our fat out of the fire.'

'What did she say, master?' Ibrahim stammered.

'She thinks you should stay,' Dakkar murmured. 'She has no common sense. Like you.'

'Please, master.' Ibrahim fell to his knees. 'I have no family. I will have to beg on the streets. If I die, no one will mourn me.'

'I will!' Dakkar said. 'You are too young!'

'He's got nobody back at that city,' Georgia said quietly, echoing Ibrahim. 'He'll end up a criminal or dead. Besides, can we waste valuable time dropping him off?'

Ibrahim looked up at him, his eyes wide and solemn. 'I will work hard and fight fiercely!'

'Oh, very well,' Dakkar said, heaving a sigh of defeat. Secretly he felt glad that Ibrahim was coming along. 'Georgia is right. Stopping at Algiers will slow us down anyway.'

With a clap of his hands, Ibrahim jumped up and scurried down into the belly of the *Nautilus*. 'Thank you, master, you won't be sorry!'

'I hope not,' Dakkar called after him.

The grey skies returned as the *Nautilus* flew across the mountains. Flying in a straight line took them far west of Algiers and across the Mediterranean to Spain and then Portugal. Dakkar watched the land below pass by.

'It all looks the same from up here,' he muttered to Georgia one day when he was steering the craft. 'One country isn't very different from another.'

'But people are,' Georgia said.

'I don't think so,' Dakkar said. 'I think most people just want to be left to get on with their lives.'

They took shifts at the helm but Ibrahim was deemed too young to fly, much to his disgust. 'You can help in the kitchen. You will make an excellent cook.' Dakkar said.

Dakkar's prediction didn't prove correct. Ibrahim managed to burn anything he tried to cook, but Fletcher and Georgia put on a brave face and ate it anyway.

'How old is he? Eight?' Georgia said, her tone chiding Dakkar, who would throw the burned offerings to the land below and eat the strips of salt beef. The goddess hardly ate anything but just stared at her plate as if she were gazing into a deep pool.

Ibrahim would look fierce. 'I am a street child, not a cook!'

The dusty brown interior of Spain gave way to green hills and vineyards, and soon they could see the sea. All this time, the goddess had lain in the guest cabin, either asleep or staring at something no one else could see on the ceiling. Georgia and Dakkar stood in her room.

'We need to try and snap her out of that trance she's in,' Georgia said. 'She hasn't eaten for days and has only taken a few sips of water.'

'I don't understand why Marek kept her,' Dakkar said, frowning.

'Well, she's purty enough,' Georgia said, sniffing dismissively. 'She was a focus. Something for the men to worship while they did Marek's dirty work for no pay.'

'I can see that, but there's something else about her,' Dakkar murmured. 'Something Marek said about her being special.' He sat down at her bedside. 'Where are you from?' he said gently, not expecting a reply.

'England,' she sighed, not looking at him. 'Green England by the sea.'

Dakkar leapt up. 'Are you awake? What's your name? How did you come to be in Marek's temple?'

'Steady, Dakkar, keep calm,' Georgia said, grabbing his arm.

'Tegen,' she said faintly, closing her eyes. 'My name is . . . Tegen.'

With a sigh, she fell asleep.

It hadn't occurred to Dakkar that finding one ship in the Atlantic Ocean would be so hard. It had taken two days to reach the sea and now he stood with Fletcher on the front deck of the *Nautilus*, scanning the steel-grey waves with a telescope.

'Most ships don't stray that far from shore, do they?' Dakkar wondered aloud.

'The trouble is, they all look the bloomin' same from up here, and who said there'd be so many of 'em?' Fletcher grumbled, squinting over the side.

'We should have thought how busy the waterways are between England and the Mediterranean,' Dakkar said, putting down his telescope.

'What about this goddess woman, Tegen?' Fletcher said, waggling his eyebrows. 'She's a rare beauty and no mistake. D'you think she could fall for a young man like me?'

Dakkar rolled his eyes. 'What? Someone with no future prospects or even a surname?' he said. 'Unlikely.'

Fletcher didn't rise to the jibe. He had returned to searching the waves with a telescope. 'You said the *Serqet* is flying the flag of the Netherlands, right Dakkar?'

'That's right. Red, white and blue with an orange pennant underneath,' Dakkar said, lifting his own telescope to his eye. 'Why?'

'Cos there's a Dutch ship just out to sea there.' Fletcher grinned. 'And HMS *Slaughter* is right close by. Looks like Commander Blizzard's about to save the day!'

Dakkar felt the blood drain from his face. 'If Blizzard so much as fires one shot at that ship, it'll explode . . .'

'Releasing the gas,' Fletcher whispered in horror.

'It'll kill everyone down there!'

CHAPTER TWENTY-THREE
DEATH PLUNGE

'We have to get down there and sink the *Serqet* before Blizzard opens fire,' Dakkar yelled, running back to the submarine's main tower and clambering up the ladder.

By the time Dakkar slid down the ladder into the control room, Georgia was letting the gas out of the balloons. 'I saw HMS *Slaughter* down there and guessed you'd want to meet up with her,' she said, grinning at Dakkar. She frowned at his pale face. 'What is it?'

'We need to descend fast, Georgia,' Dakkar said. 'That's the *Serqet* down there, and it looks like HMS *Slaughter* is about to give her a broadside . . .'

'Oh my. If we can ram the *Serqet*, she'll sink without an explosion,' Georgia murmured and frowned at the controls. 'But I can't speed up the deflation of the balloons . . .'

'I can,' Dakkar said.

Fletcher had joined them now, but Dakkar turned and began climbing up the ladder to the outside world again.

'Dakkar, no!' Georgia shouted, but Dakkar just ignored her and leapt down on to the front deck, drawing his scimitar. He ran forward and slashed at the foremost balloon and the cables holding it gave way with a twang. The submarine jolted forward and the surface of the sea and the two ships bounced into view. Dakkar stumbled, grabbing the rail that ran around the front deck. He swung his blade at another balloon, sending it hissing into the air. The sea was beginning to rush up to meet them now. The deck hung from the rear balloons at a crazy angle and Dakkar wondered if he would be able to run back up it to the safety of the tower.

The wood of the deck felt smooth and steep as Dakkar powered up it towards the middle of the submarine. His thighs burned and his feet thumped against the deck in time with his beating heart. He could feel the cold wind whipping through his thick, black hair as the sub plummeted towards the sea. With a yell, he leapt towards the tower, which hurtled at him, grabbing the rail at its top and swinging inside the tower. He barely had time to shut the hatch when, with a deafening BOOM, the *Nautilus* dived into the water.

The craft levelled out, sending Dakkar tumbling down into the control room on top of Fletcher.

'Woohoo!' Georgia screeched as she slammed the submarine into *Full Ahead* and powered towards the hull of the *Serqet*. 'Target directly ahead, Dakkar!'

'You're bloomin' barmy, d'you know that?' Fletcher

gabbled, untangling himself from Dakkar and staggering to his feet. 'Barmy!'

Dakkar grinned. 'I know!' he said. 'And it's "you're bloomin' barmy, *your highness*" to you!'

'I suggest you stop the smart talk and hold on to something,' Georgia said. 'The *Serqet*'s hull is coming up fast!'

The dark silhouette of the ship grew bigger and bigger. Dakkar had rammed a ship once before in the heat of battle with disastrous results. But that was in a smaller version of the *Nautilus*. Even now he felt his stomach churn as they drew nearer. He gripped the back of Georgia's seat and braced himself as the side of the ship filled their vision. For one brief second, Dakkar glimpsed barnacles, seaweed clinging to the wood, even a few nail heads glimmering in the murky green twilight. Then the metal-covered beak of the submarine crashed into the hull with another huge THUMP. The sharp crack of timbers and the sound of rushing water surrounded them. Objects thumped against the side of the submarine. Then a second impact threw Dakkar forward as they powered through the other side of the hull.

'Oh my!' Georgia shouted, dragging the pilot wheel to the left as the side of HMS *Slaughter* appeared before them. Dakkar found himself falling over Fletcher as the top of the submersible scraped along the keel of the ship. 'I hadn't realised she was so close!'

Georgia wrestled with the submarine, slowing her down and bringing her to a halt. Dakkar scrambled to his feet and helped Fletcher up. The control room was filled with their panting.

Somewhere below they heard Ibrahim cursing in Turkish and kicking out at something. 'What are you doing up there? Trying to kill me?'

Dakkar smirked and caught Georgia's eye. Soon she began to laugh and Fletcher joined in, filling the room with hysterical, relieved laughter.

Ibrahim popped up from the hatch below. His turban sat loosely at an angle on his head and he scowled at them. His face was covered in flour. 'I was just about to try and bake some bread!'

Dakkar helped him up into the cabin and dusted him down. 'Sorry, Ibrahim, there was no time to warn you.' He turned to Georgia. 'You'd better bring her to the surface. Commander Blizzard will be wondering what's happened.'

Georgia nodded and blew the water from the hollow hull that kept them submerged. Dakkar gave a faint smile at the feel of the submarine bobbing on the water. They watched as the sea bubbled around them, slowly giving way to daylight through the window that filled the front of the tower.

As they sailed towards HMS *Slaughter*, debris from the wrecked *Serqet* bumped against their sides. Dakkar could see broken lengths of mast, a few barrels, rope and planks swirling around on the choppy surface of the sea. The waves rocked the *Nautilus* and Dakkar's stomach lifted. *Back where I belong*, he thought.

'Looks like we stopped the cargo from exploding,' he said. 'Let's go up top and greet Commander Blizzard.'

'He's goin' to be pleased to see us and no mistake,' Fletcher said, grinning. Dakkar smiled back. He liked the commander but Fletcher idolised him. Blizzard had pulled Fletcher from a life of thieving in London's notorious Holy Land. He'd do anything to please the commander.

'Why is the world moving?' Ibrahim groaned, clutching his stomach. 'I don't like it.'

'You'll get used to it,' Georgia said, grinning at him.

'Why is she laughing at me?' Ibrahim said, pulling a face.

'She isn't,' Dakkar said. 'She feels sorry for you.'

'But everything is moving,' Ibrahim wailed.

Dakkar smiled. 'The best feeling in the world,' he said and turned to the ladder that led outside.

They climbed up out of the *Nautilus*'s tower and waved to the men working on HMS *Slaughter*. Bells rang on the deck and a line of red-coated marines stood along the side of the ship.

There was little debris now. A few spars of wood and a forlorn piece of sail bobbed on the water, but there was no other sign of the ship that had carried Marek's deadly cargo.

'Looks like we did a thorough job,' Dakkar said, but something squirmed in his stomach as he surveyed what little wreckage there was. And he couldn't think why.

Soon a team of men from the ship rowed Dakkar and Georgia over to HMS *Slaughter*. Blizzard met them on the mid deck. The scar running down his pale cheek looked white in the cold daylight. He didn't seem happy to see them.

He didn't look happy at all.

CHAPTER TWENTY-FOUR

SLAUGHTER ON THE SEA

'Dakkar,' Blizzard said, narrowing his eyes. 'I think the first time we met at sea I asked you why I shouldn't take you and hang you like a common pirate. I find myself asking the same question again.'

'I don't understand, commander,' Dakkar said, taking a step torwards him. The guards surrounding him leapt forward, pointing their bayonets and loaded rifles at Dakkar and Georgia. Dakkar glanced at the marines. He didn't recognise any of them. Normally there were one or two familiar faces, men he had fought with at the battle of Waterloo or crew from the Greenland adventure, but all of these men stared back at him with deadly indifference.

Blizzard's icy blue eyes glittered with rage. 'I received an urgent message from James Clark-Ross telling me you'd been accused of murdering Chudwell,' he said, barely controlling the anger in his voice. 'I also hear you attacked a senior judge and escaped from court. Now you ram the *Nautilus* into that Algerian vessel, very nearly sinking us in the process!'

'The *Serqet* was no innocent ship, commander,' Georgia burst out. 'She was carrying a deadly cargo and if you'd bombarded them with your cannon, you'd all be dead now.'

Blizzard said nothing but stared at the two of them for what seemed like an eternity.

'Commander, maybe we should explain,' Dakkar said, breaking the silence at last. 'Perhaps we could retire to the privacy of your cabin. You'll soon see our innocence, I promise you!'

Still Blizzard said nothing. He seemed to be in deep thought. Finally he gave a grunt and turned towards his cabin door. 'Let them follow,' he said to the guards, who lowered their weapons.

It took some time to tell Blizzard everything that had happened. Dakkar told some of the story and Georgia filled in relevant details as he went along. Blizzard sat at his desk in his cabin, twirling a glass of port and listening, his eyes gleaming.

'I wish I had been there, Dakkar,' he said, leaning forward. 'Marek Oginski dead, you say?'

'And the temple destroyed,' Dakkar added, with a sigh. 'We rescued the woman he was using as a living goddess to command the men. But we nearly lost the ship carrying the poison gas.'

Blizzard set his glass down on the desk in front of him. 'That's safely taken care of, thanks to you,' he said. 'It was pure coincidence that we met with the *Serqet*. Clark-Ross had communicated some of your story about the men with the scorpion tattoos and the name of the ship. When we spotted her, I couldn't believe my luck, but of course we were only just preparing to board her when you sank the ship.'

'I shudder to think what might have happened if we hadn't intervened,' Georgia said. 'Will the gas be safe down there?'

'A few fish may die but I imagine it would take a great deal more of Marek's poison to contaminate the wide ocean,' Blizzard said. 'It looks like the case is closed on another of the brothers Oginski. Now, this woman you rescued. Who is she?'

Dakkar shrugged. 'Your guess is as good as mine,' he said. 'Her real name is Tegen but she's in some kind of stupor and hardly speaks.'

'She needs food and more water,' Georgia added. 'She's weak from all the potions Marek fed her to keep her in line.'

'Bring her aboard,' Blizzard said, examining the cruel barb on the hook that replaced his hand. 'The doctor can look at her.'

'I think she's better where she is,' Georgia said.

A flash of irritation twisted Blizzard's face. 'And why is that?' he snapped. Dakkar had forgotten that the man liked to be in charge. He was a fair man but ruled with a rod of iron and had the total loyalty of his men. A complete contrast to Marek, who used blind faith, or the other Oginskis, who had ruled by fear and cruelty.

'Well, she's a fine-looking, grown woman to start with,' Georgia said, her face reddening. 'Not a slip of a girl like me, who can pass for a cabin boy sometimes.'

Dakkar grinned and felt himself blushing too. There was no way Georgia could be mistaken for anything other than a young woman these days.

Georgia frowned at him. 'Besides,' she continued, 'she's too weak to get on board. She's liable to fall in the sea.'

'We could winch her over,' Blizzard murmured. 'She might have useful information. Remember, we have destroyed their leader but Marek's army of rabble-rousers is still active in London. They could still cause a lot of bloodshed. She might know names of ringleaders, places they meet, anything that might help us avert an attempted revolution.'

'I don't think she knows anything,' Dakkar said. 'Even if she overheard any names, she's too addled to help us. She's only just been able to tell us her own name.'

'She's too weak to move,' Georgia said, frowning. 'We shouldn't be swinging her over the side of a ship like a barrel of salt beef.'

Blizzard smirked and inclined his head. 'As you wish, young lady. If you feel she doesn't pose any threat,' he said. 'I can have the doctor hoisted over to the *Nautilus* more easily. Although he's more adept at sawing off limbs and sewing up wounds than fixing troubled minds. To be honest, the ship is full to the gunwales anyway. I'm not sure I could offer her or your good selves a berth to sleep in.' Blizzard gazed at his hook again and picked up his port glass with his good hand, draining it in one gulp. 'It's time to get you back to England and clear your name, Dakkar,' he said.

Dakkar sighed. 'You make it sound so simple. But we have no witnesses and I think my escape will prejudice my case . . .'

'Trust me, Dakkar,' Blizzard said, raising his good hand. 'When you get back to London, true justice will be served. Have no fear. I'll have the doctor sent over. If you could ask Mr Fletcher to join me at his earliest convenience.'

The doctor accompanied them back to the *Nautilus*. Fletcher had brought her alongside and, with the help of HMS *Slaughter*'s crew, had rigged up a hoist to make getting across to the submersible easier.

Once inside, the doctor couldn't hide his wonder. He stared at the pipes and cables that snaked around the captain's cabin and gazed out of the windows.

'I'd love to see the view out of there when she's underwater,' he said, polishing his glasses and squinting through the glass again, as if imagining the shoals of fish and swaying seaweed.

Georgia gave an impatient cough. 'The patient is down here, doctor,' she said pointedly. 'We can give you a tour later if you wish.'

Tegen lay in the cabin, her breathing shallow, her

eyes staring at the low ceiling. It felt stuffy and airless in the tiny room, especially with the three of them crammed in.

The doctor checked her pulse and got her to sit up. Tegen still stared ahead listlessly. She blinked when the doctor passed his bony hand in front of her eyes. He shook his head.

'She's beyond my help. Who knows what poisons Marek has been feeding her. She is quite addled,' he said sadly. 'Maybe she can take some broth. Keep her warm. I'll recommend to Commander Blizzard that we take her to an asylum when we reach England.'

Tegen blinked and turned her head to the doctor, making him start. 'England,' she said. 'Green and . . . and . . .' Tears welled in her eyes and she grabbed the doctor's arm. 'Don't let him. Stop him.'

Georgia leapt forward, holding Tegen's arms. 'Easy, ma'am,' she said, her voice low and soothing. 'Easy now.'

Tegen stared into the shadows of the cabin, terrified. 'He mustn't . . . mustn't . . .' She fell back on to the bed with a long, chilling scream.

The doctor turned away. 'I'll report back to the commander,' he said. 'If she does have some knowledge of Marek's plans, then it's locked deep within her mind and out of our reach.'

Dakkar showed the doctor back to the hoist in silence, neither of them mentioning a tour or demonstration. Tegen's outburst had unsettled them both. Just as he climbed into the hoist to take him back to the ship, the doctor turned and fixed Dakkar with a hard stare.

'Keep her safe,' he said. 'If she does know something, however lost in the corridors of her mind, then her life is at risk. Guard her well.'

'She's on the *Nautilus*, in the shadow of HMS *Slaughter*,' Dakkar said. 'She couldn't be safer.'

'Maybe,' the doctor said, and signalled for the sailors on the ship to winch him over.

Frowning, Dakkar wandered back to Tegen's cabin, where Georgia sat at her bedside. Tegen had fallen into a troubled sleep and was murmuring and tossing her head. Sweat beaded her brow and Georgia dabbed at her face with a damp cloth.

She looked up at him with a pale face. 'We can't let them put her in an asylum,' she said. 'Have you seen those places?'

Dakkar let out a long breath. 'No, but I've heard tell of them,' he growled. 'We can't allow that, but where can she stay?'

'Why not with us?' Georgia said.

'She can't live on the *Nautilus*!' Dakkar said, staring at Georgia incredulously.

'I didn't mean on here!' Georgia said. 'You have means enough to have her cared for in London. She could lodge with us. I'm sure she'll recover with the right care.'

'Not him,' Tegen groaned and she rolled over, sobbing.

'Do you think it was Marek being mentioned that upset her?' Georgia said, mouthing the name 'Marek' so as not to upset Tegen again.

Dakkar shrugged. 'It could be,' he said. He paused, thinking. 'But it was strange when she started crying out. I can't think why, but something seems odd to me.'

'Anyone who's met an Oginski would end up having bad dreams,' Georgia said and shuddered. 'It's a wonder *we* can sleep at night.'

'Fletcher can make some fish broth and we'll see what we can do for her,' Dakkar said. 'We'll take it in turns to watch over her.'

Georgia looked around the cabin theatrically. 'You think she's in danger here?'

'I don't know why but I think we're all in danger,' Dakkar said. 'There's something that doesn't feel right. The sooner we get to London, the better.'

CHAPTER TWENTY-FIVE
DARK SUSPICIONS

The *Nautilus* stayed tethered to the back of HMS *Slaughter* as they sailed for England. Dakkar, Georgia and Fletcher moved between ship and submersible, dining with Blizzard and enjoying the slightly less cramped conditions on the ship. But one of them always stayed on board with Ibrahim and Tegen.

Tegen's condition improved in the next two days. She was able to take the broth that Fletcher had prepared from fish caught by lines that trailed from the stern. Ibrahim enjoyed hauling the fish in with him and didn't seem at all offended that Fletcher had taken his job.

'So, how fares your damsel in distress, Dakkar?' Blizzard asked at dinner, after a day's sailing. 'Has she come to her senses at all? Has she said anything useful?'

'No,' Dakkar said. 'She sits up and takes some of Fletcher's broth but says nothing.'

Georgia nodded in agreement. 'She looks very pale and sickly,' she said. 'Like she's recovering from a fever.'

'And who is with her now?' Blizzard asked.

'Fletcher,' Dakkar said.

Georgia suppressed a giggle. 'If you ask me, I think the boy is trying to impress her,' she said.

Blizzard pulled a disapproving face. 'Send him over to me this evening,' Blizzard said. 'I'll put him straight on a few matters . . .'

Georgia looked alarmed. 'I was only joking, commander,' she said. 'Fletcher is the perfect gentleman, I promise you!'

Blizzard narrowed his eyes. 'Nevertheless,' he said. 'I need to have a word with him.'

Fletcher stood on the deck of the *Nautilus* when they returned. 'Blizzard wants another word,' Dakkar said, nodding up at the ship.

Fletcher's face dropped. He looked past Dakkar at HMS *Slaughter*. 'Righto,' he said, and got the crew to hoist him up almost as soon as Georgia had landed.

'What's up with him?' Georgia said.

'I don't know, but Blizzard seems to be giving him a tough time,' Dakkar said.

'Maybe he blames Fletcher for letting you get into trouble,' Georgia suggested.

Dakkar shook his head. 'No, Blizzard knows that Fletcher isn't my nursemaid. If he should be angry with anyone, it should be Clark-Ross, who more or less condemned me as he tried to speak up for me.'

Dakkar found Tegen sitting up in bed when he entered her cabin. She still had a sleepy, dreamlike look on her face but shadows ringed her eyes and her skin looked greyish from lack of sunlight. There had been an unspoken agreement between Dakkar and Georgia not to mention Marek again, and Tegen still spoke little but listened to them as they told her the news of outside, the weather or what Ibrahim had been up to.

'You look well,' Dakkar said. 'How are you feeling?'

'Much better,' Tegen said, not looking at him, that strange haunted smile playing around her lips.

'You might benefit from some sea air,' Dakkar said. 'You could come up top and take a breath. I couldn't live without it.'

'I dreamt I was flying,' she said. 'Sailing above the clouds.'

'You were,' Dakkar said, then clamped his mouth shut, half hoping he didn't have to explain the *Nautilus*'s capabilities to her. In this half-drowsy state, she'd never understand.

Tegen didn't seem to notice. 'Sea air,' she said, frowning. 'Taking the air. We used to stand on the cliffs and watch the gulls.'

Dakkar stood silently, trying not to break her line of thought.

'The waves would crash below,' she said, smiling fondly into her cradled hands. 'The wind would blow and whip my hair around my face.'

'Where did the wind blow so hard?' Dakkar said gently.

She glanced at him as if noticing him for the first time. 'Cornwall,' she said. 'England by the sea. Where the wind blows hard. But no more. No more.' Her face creased and a tear trickled down her cheek. 'No more.'

'I lived in Cornwall,' Dakkar said, kneeling beside her bed. 'On a cliff top.'

A line creased her smooth brow. 'In a tall tower high above the flat moors. All gone. All gone.'

Dakkar gasped. 'How did you know that?' He leaned closer and gripped her hand. 'How could you know about the castle?'

Tears streamed down her cheeks and she pulled her hand away. 'My home,' she sobbed, throwing herself on to her pillow.

Georgia appeared at the doorway and grabbed Dakkar's arm. 'What are you doing?' she hissed. 'Look at the poor woman. She's hysterical. What did you say?'

'She said she lived in the . . . castle . . . in Cornwall . . .' Dakkar stammered. 'Georgia, I have to know more. Is she just rambling? How did she know it had been destroyed?'

'Out,' Georgia said, bundling him through the door. 'She's had enough. She's weak. She'll tell us in her own good time.'

'But how could she know?' Dakkar insisted, trying to step forward. 'Where does she come from?'

'Enough!' Georgia said, pushing Dakkar back. 'Or do I have to sock you?'

Dakkar's shoulders slumped and the fire left him. 'I'm sorry,' he said. 'But what she was talking about . . .'

'We'll get to the bottom of that,' Georgia said, lowering her voice and closing the cabin door behind her. 'But not right away.'

Dakkar clambered up out of the submersible and sat on the tower, letting the sea breeze ruffle his hair. A few stars broke through the clouds, casting shadows on the water. A bell rang on the silhouette of HMS *Slaughter* and he could hear crew members moving about on the ship. *Was Tegen in league with Marek in some way?* Dakkar thought. *Was she there, spying on the castle as I grew up? But she said she lived there.* It was like some horrible puzzle that Dakkar didn't have all the pieces for and couldn't fit together.

At some point, Dakkar's confused thoughts calmed and he watched the wake of the submarine, gleaming white in the pale starlight. Soothed by the rocking creak of the craft and the swish of the waves on its bow, he dozed off, leaning on the wall of the tower.

Dakkar woke with a start. His stomach lurched and he knew immediately that something was wrong. The motion of the *Nautilus* felt different. Instead of the side-to-side roll of being towed, the craft pitched back and forth. He stood up and his head throbbed.

'We've been cut adrift,' Dakkar said, scanning the dark sea for any sign of HMS *Slaughter* or anything else. Nothing. Without hesitating, Dakkar leapt down the ladder into the tower and the dark control room. The captain's seat was empty. Dakkar sniffed. An unfamiliar bitter smell hung in the air.

'Georgia?' Dakkar called into the body of the submersible. 'Fletcher? Ibrahim?'

No reply.

The oil lamps that normally glowed in brackets on the walls were all snuffed out. Only the blue flicker of the Voltalith, the electrically charged meteorite that powered the submersible, lit the main corridor of the ship, casting long shadows against the varnished wood from within the engine room. Dakkar held his breath.

Someone was moving around in there.

He slid along the passage, pressing himself against the wall, stopping when his foot brushed something. Looking down, he stifled a yell. Ibrahim lay staring up at him through lifeless eyes. Dakkar swallowed hard and crouched down, lifting the boy's heavy head. His skin felt cold. Tears prickled the back of Dakkar's eyes as he remembered Ibrahim begging to be allowed to come. Wiping his face roughly, he lay the boy down on the floor gently, strode down the corridor and peered into the engine room.

This space was as large as the stern of the submersible. Wires and pipes twisted and snaked their way around it and dangled from the ceiling in places, obscuring the view of the whole space. In the centre, wrapped in a nest of cables, sat a blue disc, a fragment of the Voltalith. Next to that stood a cast-iron furnace, again criss-crossed by copper piping and tubes that superheated the fuel inside. Steam blew from the furnace.

A thick main pipe ran from the furnace to the wall. This filled the balloons with hot air. Georgia lay slumped over it, face down. Someone moved from behind a dangling cluster of cables. Dakkar turned and saw stars as something heavy and metal clipped his brow. The room spun and darkness took him.

Dakkar's head pulsed and throbbed. The side of his head felt warm and sticky, and as he forced his eyelids open, he realised his hands were tied. He tried to clear his head, groaning at the pain that lanced between his eyes.

Wild shadows danced across the walls of the engine room and sparks arced across the space. A figure stood silhouetted against the dazzling light. Whoever it was had been pulling wires and ripping pipes from the walls.

'Who are you?' Dakkar croaked. 'What's going on?'

The figure spun round at the sound of Dakkar's voice and he found himself staring straight into the wide, frightened eyes of Fletcher.

CHAPTER TWENTY-SIX
TREACHERY AND FEAR

At first Dakkar just stared at Fletcher, not able to take in the sight of him feverishly pulling the *Nautilus*'s engine to pieces.

'Fletcher, what are you doing?' Dakkar said, struggling at the ropes that bound his wrists.

Fletcher didn't look at Dakkar. 'Don't talk to me. I've got to do this. I'm sorry, Dakkar, but I 'ave to.'

'What are you talking about? Why are you pulling the engine apart? Why did you kill Ibrahim?'

'He ain't dead,' he said. 'Just paralysed. Used some poison gas on him. Georgia too. He'll be right as rain in a while . . .' Fletcher's face dropped. 'Well . . . for a bit . . .'

'What are you talking about, Fletcher? I thought you were on our side, Project Nemo's bright hope!' Dakkar said.

Fletcher pulled an anguished face. 'Maybe that's what this is,' he said, ripping another cable out. Tears streamed down his cheeks. 'Maybe I've got to prove myself . . .'

'You don't want to do this, Fletcher, I can tell,' Dakkar said. 'What's got into you?'

Fletcher stopped and scrubbed his face furiously. 'You're my friend, Dax,' he said. 'But orders is orders and I've been told . . .'

'Orders? Who from?' Dakkar said.

Fletcher shook his head slowly and he began to cry again. 'I can't say,' he said. 'I've just got to disable the ship. I was hoping to knock you all out. Make it look like some kind of accident so when you woke up you wouldn't know it was me . . .'

'Who's put you up to this?' Dakkar demanded. 'Voychek Oginski?'

'I can't say,' Fletcher said, his voice quavering. 'I can't go against 'im.'

'Don't be afraid, Fletcher. Together we are stronger than anyone,' Dakkar said. 'We're the lads from Project Nemo. Think what we've been through together!'

Fletcher stopped and walked over to Dakkar. 'I'm sorry, Dax, but there's no other way.'

'You're mad,' Dakkar said, desperately pulling at the tight ropes that held him. 'You can't do this.'

Fletcher turned back to Dakkar and opened his mouth to say something. A swift movement behind him caught Dakkar's eye. A loud clunk followed and Fletcher fell on top of Dakkar, revealing Tegen's worried face.

'Is this . . . real?' she said, her eyes flickering from one part of the room to another. She peered hard at Dakkar. 'You're bleeding.'

Dakkar gave a weak smile. 'I'll be fine. If you can untie me, I'll be a lot better.'

Georgia and Ibrahim lay in their cabins, sleeping off the worst of the gas. Fletcher was still unconscious, bound and gagged in his room. Dakkar sat beside the sabotaged engine, flinching as the Voltalith spat and fizzed.

'Can you fix it?' Tegen said, dabbing a damp cloth on the gash at the side of his head. In her white nightgown with her wild hair, she looked like some kind of ghost.

'I'm not sure. Weren't you affected by the gas?' he asked her, wincing as she dabbed a damp cloth on the wound.

'It seems not,' she said. 'My cabin door was shut.'

Dakkar wondered if she'd been exposed to so many toxins and poisons that somehow she'd become immune. He knew of a fakir back in India who said he'd been bitten by so many snakes that he could no longer be poisoned. Maybe it was like that.

'Why did Fletcher turn against us?' Dakkar wondered aloud. 'He seemed scared. What hold would anyone have over him? The only person I can imagine who could instil such fear would be an Oginski. And the only Oginski left alive is Voychek.' It was only slight, but Dakkar noticed Tegen flinch with the cloth. He looked up at her. 'You know the name?'

She blanched, swallowing hard and not meeting his

eye. 'I know Voychek Oginski,' she said coldly. 'And if I ever meet him, then he will die.'

'They say he is a master of disguise,' Dakkar said, taking the cloth and holding it to his head.

'I'll know him when I see him. I left my mark,' she said. Her anger ebbed away and the sad, faraway look returned. 'We lived in Cornwall on the cliffs. Our home was called the castle but really it was just a tower with a few outbuildings.'

A thousand questions boiled to the surface of Dakkar's mind but he bit his tongue, forcing them to stay unspoken so that the story could be told. 'Who did you live there with?'

'My mother and father and my brother,' she said. 'We were richer than many of the poor folk around those parts but we weren't wealthy. Mother and father were religious people. They disapproved of and shunned high society.'

'So you were unknown, in other words,' Dakkar said, realisation dawning on him. 'Isolated from the rest of the world.'

'We had little to do with the villagers,' she said. 'Nothing to do with other local gentry. But my brother, John, was so ambitious. He wanted to be an officer in the navy. Father and he often argued about it. My father was a pacifist, you see.'

'So your brother left?'

Tegen swallowed back a sob. 'He intended to, but the Oginskis found us before that,' she said. 'They came in the night with men and guns. We were unarmed, defenceless. They slaughtered my parents.' Tears trickled down her cheeks and she sobbed. 'My brother put up a fight but Voychek beat him to the ground and killed him. He was laughing as he did it. I'll never forget the evil in his cold, pale eyes.'

Dakkar's mouth was dry. She was describing how the Oginskis took the castle. Was *his* Oginski, Franciszek, involved? How could he not be if he lived there for so many years?

He barely dared to ask the question. 'Was there another brother there? A tall man, not as big as Marek but . . .'

Tegen shook her head. 'All I know is that Voychek and Marek killed my family. I saw them for certain and Marek took me as a slave. And that's where I've been all these years. Marek kept me a secret from his brother, knowing that I would recognise Voychek if I saw him again and keeping me as a safeguard.'

Dakkar nodded. 'Marek said something about you being able to see through the most ingenious disguise.'

'But it wasn't Voychek Oginski that Marek had to be worried about, was it?' Tegen said. She scowled. 'I'm glad he died.'

Dakkar remained silent. *Oginski must have been given the castle by his brothers while he was still with Cryptos*, he thought. *How could he live there, knowing its murderous past?*

He fought these thoughts away. 'You said you would recognise Voychek if you saw him. How?'

'There are some things you can't disguise,' Tegen began, but Dakkar held up a hand to silence her and listened.

A muffled tapping came through the ceiling of the room, rattling across the planks of the deck like many tiny feet.

'We have company,' Dakkar hissed. 'And I left the tower hatch open.' He glanced around, searching for a weapon, and came upon a hammer that Fletcher had used to smash some of the components of the engine.

He crept up the passage, casting a long shadow in the blue light from the engine room. The clattering feet didn't sound human. They reminded him of insects or the scorpions at Marek's temple. He shuddered.

A thin shaft of starlight shone down from the top of the tower into the central passage. If anything came in, it would be through there, but beyond that beam of light was the armoury at the bow of the submersible. It was where the sea arrows lay, and the rifles and pistols.

The bony clicking grew louder.

Tegen crouched behind Dakkar. 'Wait here,' he said. 'I'm going to get something a bit more effective than this.' He held up the hammer and scurried towards the front of the craft.

Dakkar reached the pool of starlight that illuminated the passage, fully intending to hurry on forward, but he stopped and glanced up.

The circular hatch framed the sky at the top of the tower. Dakkar felt as though he was at the bottom of a deep well, looking up. The brass wheels and dials in the control room gleamed faintly, as did the polished rungs of the ladder leading to the outside. Dakkar glimpsed an antenna and heard the rattle of claws on wood.

Then a black shape blotted out the sky. Dakkar felt a heavy weight on his head; sharp, spiny claws wrapped around his face and the smell of the sea filled his senses. With a muffled scream, Dakkar fell back to the floor as another weight hit his chest. Whatever it was had just landed on him and was intent on tearing his face off.

CHAPTER TWENTY-SEVEN

CRAWLERS FROM THE DEEP

Sharp spines scored at Dakkar's cheeks, probing at his eyes and mouth. Something else stabbed at his chest and ribs. Keeping his mouth and eyes squeezed shut, he pounded his fists on the creature that had wrapped itself around his face. His knuckles hit hard shell.

Dakkar had no idea what had clung to him. He could feel many spiny legs scraping at his skin, and plates of armour undulated in his grip. Rolling over on to his front, he managed to get on to his knees and slammed his head on to the floor. Flashes of light blossomed in his darkened sight but he did it again, feeling the creature loosen its grip. He grabbed the thing with both his hands and pulled, tearing it away from his face.

In the dim light, Dakkar could see the underbelly of some kind of multi-legged nightmare. It reminded him of a woodlouse, the kind of thing he had found under a stone back at the castle when he was younger. He could see its pale, segmented body and the rows of legs waving frantically, trying to tear at his flesh.

With a yell of disgust, he slammed it on the floor, hearing the satisfying crunch of its shell. It lay still, but another was clawing its way up his body towards his head. Dakkar ripped it from him and grasped its waving feelers, swinging it over his head and smashing it on the ground.

Another fell on his back and another landed at his feet. He stamped on one and crashed backward against the wall of the submersible again and again. More of the creatures fell through the hatch, their pale bodies writhing as they pushed themselves on to their feet. He could see the plates of shell striping their backs.

Dakkar cried out and, snatching up the hammer from the floor, smashed down on them, striking and kicking left and right. Tegen charged forward with what looked like a heavy frying pan but was actually a shovel for the furnace.

She clanged it down, crushing and splattering the creatures. More and more of them fell into the passage, pushing Dakkar and Tegen back towards the armoury. Dakkar breathed a prayer of thanks that he'd shut the cabin doors on the others, so they were in no immediate danger.

The passage floor crawled with the creatures now and Dakkar dragged Tegen into the armoury and slammed the door, slicing one of the things neatly in two. The front half fell into the room with them, twisting and skittering on the floor until the light faded from its bulbous eyes.

'What are they?' Tegen panted.

Dakkar put a hand to his face. 'Some kind of crawlers from the bottom of the sea.' He looked at the blood on his fingers. 'Vicious brutes too.'

Tegen looked around. 'Can we use anything in here to kill them?'

Dakkar rummaged through boxes and overturned barrels. 'Any kind of explosion inside the *Nautilus* would be disastrous. There's gas for the balloons, heat from the furnace, the electricity from the Voltalith, not to mention the gunpowder in here.'

A scratching, gnawing sound came from the bottom of the door. 'They're going to get through before long,' Tegen said, looking pale.

Snatching up a clear bottle, Dakkar looked at the label.

'What's that?' Tegen said.

'Acid,' Dakkar replied. 'At the back of the *Nautilus* we have sepia bombs, glass globes full of thick ink that will create a black cloud in the water if we need to escape or confuse a pursuer. We use acid in the sepia cloud to make it a little more . . . potent as a weapon.'

'There's another bottle here,' Tegen said. 'Is it safe to use?'

'We don't have much choice,' Dakkar said. 'Load a couple of pistols and get your shovel ready. I'll open the door and throw this into the middle of them but the front ones will have to be dealt with.'

They loaded their weapons and Dakkar found a boat hook on a long pole. He readied himself by the door.

'On my count of three,' he said. 'One, two, three!' Dakkar yanked the door open.

The corridor undulated with the crawlers as they scrambled over each other to get to Dakkar. The liquid rained down on the seething mass and a foul stench of burning filled the passage. Those at the centre of the passage writhed and squirmed as the acid ate into them, but the nearest ones scuttled forward. Tegen fired a pistol, then another and another, sending three crawlers flying back. Dakkar grabbed the second bottle and smashed it just in front of him. The creatures hit by the acid tried to roll up into a ball but the liquid burned into their armour.

Tegen smashed her shovel down, killing two more, and Dakkar began to stab and harass the crawlers behind them. The monsters were slowly forced back, their feet melting in the acid that pooled on the floor.

Dakkar grabbed two more loaded pistols and fired them, managing to kill a third creature when the bullet went straight through the first. His boots crunched on dead crawlers as he strode forward, kicking and stamping on anything that moved. Three creatures remained, and Tegen cut one in half with her shovel.

With a final yell, Dakkar stabbed his boathook through one and stamped hard on the last. Only the occasional crack of shells, and the hissing of the acid as it liquefied the dead crawlers, broke the silence.

'I'd better check the tower and shut us in,' he said. 'We need some water too to douse the floor.'

Georgia's cabin door swung open and she peered out,

her face screwed up as if she'd just emerged from a long night's sleep.

'What's going on?' she said, rubbing her eyes. 'And what's that disgusting smell?'

Dakkar finally managed to get the engine working, but their progress was slow and the Voltalith wasn't giving full power. The ship stank of acid and dead sea-crawlers, and Dakkar was anxious that the acid might still be damaging the floor and eating its way towards the hollow hull. They were unable to submerge because all the power they had was being used to drive them forward. The water of the English Channel flashed by them, but they had to avoid being seen by too many ships and so had to constantly watch out and change their course.

Tegen stood staring out to sea, hoping to catch a first glimpse of England. Georgia and Ibrahim stood speechless in the control room, listening to Dakkar as he explained all that had happened with Fletcher and the crawlers.

'Why?' Georgia said.

Dakkar held his hands up. 'I wish I knew. He sounded afraid. He was talking as if somebody had some kind of hold over him, and the appearance of those crawling things could only mean one thing . . .'

'Cryptos,' Georgia murmured. 'But why turn on us now? When Marek's plot is defeated . . .'

'Unless it isn't just Marek's plot,' Dakkar said, feeling the blood drain from his face.

'And the plot isn't foiled yet,' Georgia whispered.

'Voychek,' Dakkar said.

Silence fell over them as they contemplated the horrible truth. 'But Fletcher must have been working for Cryptos all along,' Georgia said at last. 'Since Blizzard picked him up off the streets. How is that possible? None of it makes any sense.'

Ibrahim's face grew long. 'I thought Fletcher was my friend,' he said.

'I'll make him talk,' Georgia said, her face darkening. Then she choked back a sob. 'I really trusted Fletcher. I thought he was one of us.'

'Where is he now, your highness?' Ibrahim asked.

'Still tied up in his room,' Dakkar said.

'You should punish him badly!' Ibrahim said, frowning. Dakkar was surprised at the depth of the little boy's feelings, but then Fletcher had been the one to show the most interest in him. Dakkar could tell Ibrahim felt deeply betrayed.

'We need to get to the bottom of why he turned on us,' Dakkar said, quickly explaining to Georgia what Ibrahim had said.

'He was Commander Blizzard's chosen man,' Georgia said. 'I . . .' She stopped in mid sentence and frowned at Tegen. 'Are you all right?'

Tegen gripped the wall, her face pale. 'What did you say about Fletcher?'

'He was selected by Commander Blizzard,' Georgia said. 'Why what's the problem?'

'That's *my* name,' she said. '*I'm* Blizzard, Tegen Blizzard.'

CHAPTER TWENTY-EIGHT
A MYSTERY DEEPENS

Tegen looked frightened. She stared hard at Dakkar, then Georgia. 'This man, Blizzard,' she said. 'Who is he? Is he your friend?'

'He's a naval commander,' Dakkar said. 'I've fought alongside him many times.'

'He's a great man,' Georgia said grudgingly. 'For a Brit. He'll get to the bottom of this. He trusted Fletcher implicitly. He'll want to know how a Cryptos spy worked himself so deeply into Project Nemo.'

Tegen trembled slightly. 'How is it he has the same name as me?' she said. 'It doesn't make sense.'

'It could be a simple coincidence,' Georgia said. 'I'd trust Commander Blizzard with my life. Isn't that right, Dakkar?'

Dakkar looked hard at Tegen. 'Yes,' he said. 'Yes, I would.'

Tegen looked puzzled for a moment but didn't ask any

other questions. 'I feel tired,' she said, and climbed down into the *Nautilus* to her cabin.

'Do you think she's telling the truth?' Georgia said, when she'd gone. 'About her name?'

Dakkar shrugged. 'Why would she lie?'

Georgia said, 'The sooner we get to Blizzard, the better.'

'Maybe we should talk to Fletcher,' Dakkar said.

They left Ibrahim steering the *Nautilus* and went down below. Fletcher sat on his bed, hands tied behind his back. He looked miserable.

'I can't tell yer who gave me the orders to scupper the ship,' Fletcher said, staring at the floor.

'Is it because of Tegen?' Georgia said. 'Did Voychek want her dead?'

Fletcher continued to look sullenly at the floor for a moment, then looked up at Dakkar with pleading eyes. 'Believe me, Dakkar, we're better off out of this battle,' he said. 'I only did it to protect you! I didn't know them things was comin' to get us. They'd have killed me too. Just get away. Hide yourself. You don't know what you're up against. He's too powerful.'

'This is a waste of time,' Georgia said. 'Lock him up and let's take him to Blizzard and get to the bottom of this.'

Tears glistened in Fletcher's eyes. 'Don't take me to Blizzard,' he said. 'I'm beggin' you. He'll have me hanged! He's not the man you think he is. There's no mercy in him!'

'You should have thought of that before you tried to scupper the *Nautilus* for Voychek,' Dakkar said coldly.

'And don't think Blizzard will be as gentle in his questioning as we've been.'

Fletcher's eyes widened as Dakkar turned away. 'Dakkar, listen to me. I'm still your friend. Don't go to Blizzard. Stay away from London. Stay away from HMS *Slaughter*. Please! It's too dangerous, believe me.'

'I'd be more inclined to believe you if you hadn't just tried to kill us all,' Dakkar said coldly and shut the door on Fletcher.

They travelled in silence for most of the time, skimming and bumping across the waves. Dakkar managed to get a little more speed out of the damaged engine but it was frustrating. The white cliffs of Dover crawled by and they were still in danger of being spotted by other seafarers.

'I still can't believe Fletcher is Voychek's spy,' Georgia said, not looking at Dakkar.

Dakkar sighed. 'Voychek must have wanted to separate us from Blizzard for some reason.'

'Yeah, to set those horrible critters on us,' Georgia said, scowling out at the sea. 'To kill us all off.'

'Or at least to kill Tegen,' Dakkar said. 'But what's her connection with the commander and why does Voychek want her dead?'

'And why didn't the commander come back for us?' Georgia said. 'He would have realised we'd gone pretty quickly.'

'He was in a hurry to get back to London, remember? Imminent rebellion and all that? He'd trust us to catch up and if we couldn't then he'd know there was nothing he could do to help us.'

Georgia shuddered. 'He can be a cold fish sometimes,' she said. 'The mission is everything to him. We forget that.'

'He's not the man we think he is,' Dakkar muttered. 'Ruthless. Cold.'

'Exactly. And Tegen knows something,' Georgia said. 'And she's not telling us.'

'I'm not sure she completely trusts us,' Dakkar replied. He looked over to Georgia. 'Apart from you, I don't know who to trust either.' The moment he said it, one of the pieces of the puzzle fell into place. 'Oh no.'

Georgia gripped Dakkar's arm. 'Dakkar, what is it?'

'We've been so stupid,' Dakkar said. 'So unobservant.'

'What do you mean? Dakkar, talk sense!'

Dakkar turned and stared into Georgia's wide eyes. 'When we sank the *Serqet*, did you see any bodies floating on the surface?'

'No, but . . .'

'Any bodies? At all?'

'There was hardly any wreckage, Dakkar. What are you getting at?'

'When you were on board HMS *Slaughter*, did you recognise any of the crew? Any of them at all?'

'I don't understand . . .'

'The *Nautilus* more or less cut the *Serqet* in half. Even if the entire crew were hidden in the hold of that ship, some of the dead would have floated up to the surface. I remember thinking there was something strange about the wreckage. It was exactly that: it was *just* wreckage . . .'

'You mean, the crew of the *Serqet* somehow overthrew the crew of HMS *Slaughter*? Took their place?' Georgia looked stunned.

'What if Voychek has somehow infiltrated the crew? Maybe Fletcher had accomplices on board. It could be any of them. Blizzard may be in mortal danger on his own ship . . .'

Georgia shook her head. 'But Blizzard would notice the change in his crew; he's not blind or stupid. He had plenty of chances to warn us too, when we went over there for dinner. Why didn't he?'

'I'm not sure,' Dakkar sighed. He turned to Georgia and held her gaze. 'They're just ideas, Georgia. But I need to check on something when we get to HMS *Slaughter*. Will you help me?'

'Of course, Dakkar.'

'Even if it seems like we're going against Project Nemo?' Dakkar said. 'Even if I ask you to turn the *Nautilus*'s firepower on our friends?'

Georgia looked worried. 'All right,' she said slowly. 'What are you up to?'

'If the crew have turned on Blizzard, then we may need to take drastic action,' he said. 'I need to know I can rely on you completely. Because I think we may have fewer friends than we thought!'

CHAPTER TWENTY-NINE
CONFRONTATION

Finally, after what seemed like an eternity of sailing, they reached the Thames. Dakkar risked submerging and ordered Ibrahim to watch the floor where the acid had spilled in case any water seeped through. HMS *Slaughter* sat at anchor in the middle of the Thames. To the north, by Westminster Palace, Dakkar could see torches and fires burning as angry crowds gathered outside the building where the government sat.

'Trouble's brewing,' he said. 'It won't be long before that crowd reaches a size that can't be controlled.'

Keeping the *Nautilus* semi-submerged so that only the very top of the tower poked above the water, Dakkar brought her close to the side of the frigate, then handed the wheel to Georgia. Tegen stood at the foot of the ladder that led up the tower and to the outside world. A deep-hooded cloak shrouded her face and body.

'We're going up there to find out what exactly is going

on,' Dakkar said. He turned to Tegen. 'You believe you could recognise Voychek again if you saw him?'

Tegen's eyes looked cold and hard. She seemed free of any confusion now. Dakkar marvelled at how bright and alert she was. 'I know it,' she said.

'What about Fletcher?' Georgia said. Fletcher stood next to Tegen with bound hands. He looked pale and miserable. 'Can you trust him?'

'I doubt it,' Dakkar replied. 'But Blizzard might have a few questions for him.'

'Please, Dakkar,' Fletcher said, visibly trembling. 'Don't take me up there. I won't let you down again. Just don't make me go back on that ship.'

'You're going to have to, Fletcher,' Dakkar said gently. 'But it'll all be over soon.' He turned to Ibrahim. 'You stay here and help the scary lady,' he said with a smile.

'If I have to,' Ibrahim said, pulling a face. 'You take care, your highness!'

'Georgia, you know what to do?' Dakkar said, producing a wax-covered tube from under his shirt. 'If I set this flare off, you ram HMS *Slaughter*.'

Georgia gave Dakkar a hard stare. 'I don't like it, Dakkar,' she said, gripping the helm and settling back into the seat. Her face softened. 'You'll all still be on board.'

'I'll only give the signal if the situation is desperate,' Dakkar said. 'Trust me.'

'If you say so.' Georgia nodded.

'Then let's go and pay Commander Blizzard a visit,'

Dakkar said, clapping his hands. 'We may be able to unravel this mystery.'

Angry shouts began to drift over the Thames as more and more people gathered by Westminster Palace. The crew of HMS *Slaughter* scurried around the deck, preparing the cannon. Dakkar couldn't see Tegen's face in the hood of the robe, but her hands trembled as she climbed out of the *Nautilus* and up the ladder that had been lowered down from the ship.

'Don't worry,' Dakkar said. 'Just keep behind me.'

Fletcher trembled even more, looking back at Dakkar from almost every rung of the ladder, silently begging him not to make him face Blizzard. Dakkar glanced back at the sea. The *Nautilus* had submerged and was turning gracefully away from HMS *Slaughter*.

At the top of the ladder, rough hands dragged Fletcher up out of view on to the deck, then Tegen, but Dakkar sprang nimbly from the top of the ladder and glanced around him. Red-coated marines surrounded him, rifles levelled, bayonets pointed at him and the other two. He looked at them closely. They looked unfamiliar, and their tunics were weather-beaten and stained by the sea. Many of them looked no different to the sailors he'd seen on the Algerian ship. One man gave Dakkar a nod and pointed to the stern of the ship with the tip of his bayonet.

'Look around you, Tegen,' Dakkar whispered. 'If you see Voychek in among the crew, just yell and point.'

He couldn't see Tegen's face in the deep hood but she nodded.

Commander Blizzard stood on the rear deck as Dakkar, Tegen and Fletcher approached him. He looked down and gave them a puzzled smile.

'Dakkar, I'm glad to see you safe and sound. I thought we'd lost you. So glad you caught up, but this is hardly the time to make introductions,' he said. 'We're readying the cannon. That mob are turning nasty. Even the cavalry won't be able to control them. We must bombard Palace Square before they break in. I don't think that young lady wants to be up here when that happens. And why is Mr Fletcher bound?'

'*He* cut us adrift, commander,' Dakkar said. 'Tried to wreck the *Nautilus*. He said he was under orders.'

Blizzard looked stony-faced. 'Under orders? Who from?'

'I'm not certain,' Dakkar replied. 'That's why I brought him back alive. I thought we could get to the truth.'

'I'll clap him in irons,' Blizzard said. 'We can deal with him later. The most important thing at the moment is . . .'

But Tegen let out a shrill scream and pulled back the hood. 'It's him!' she yelled, pointing. 'It's Voychek Oginski!'

Dakkar felt the blood drain from his face. Tegen pointed directly at Commander Blizzard.

'Is this the mad woman you rescued from Marek's temple?' Blizzard said, his voice flat. 'Why did you bring her on deck? She'll unnerve the crew. Take her away immediately.'

Dakkar didn't move. 'You are John Blizzard, aren't you? Of the Cornwall Blizzards?' he said.

'What kind of a ridiculous question is that?' Blizzard scoffed.

'Then why don't you recognise your own sister? Tegen Blizzard?' Dakkar snapped. 'Aren't you pleased to see her?'

'This is preposterous,' Blizzard said, his scarred face twisted into a scowl.

'I know him,' Tegen said. 'I made that mark myself with a knife.' She drew a finger down the side of her face, indicating the line of Blizzard's scar. 'He killed my family and took my brother's identity!'

'Guards, take this lunatic away!' Blizzard's voice was shrill.

Dakkar stood close to her and drew his sword. 'Then tell me, "Commander Blizzard", where were you born? Where did you grow up? What were your mother and father's names?' His voice was rising now. He felt tears stinging the backs of his eyes. 'Tell me!'

Blizzard stood staring coldly at Dakkar, his lips pursed and his good hand on the handle of his pistol.

'You can't tell me because you *aren't* John Blizzard at all,' Dakkar said, his voice hoarse. 'And this isn't your sister because *you* are Voychek Oginski!'

Blizzard gave a long sigh and pulled his pistol from his belt. 'Tie them up,' he said, pointing the gun at Dakkar.

CHAPTER THIRTY
THE TRUTH

Dakkar struggled against the ropes that bound his hands behind his back. He could feel the flare tucked in his belt under his shirt. Tegen stood beside him, similarly bound. They leaned against the mainmast in the centre of the ship while men hurried about them, shifting cannonballs and kegs of powder. Across the water on the north bank of the Thames, the shouting had grown to a furious rumble, punctuated by gunshots and screams.

'My ragged army of rioters have started their work,' Voychek said, smiling. 'Soon it will all be over and Cryptos will reign supreme in this land.'

Fletcher stood, white-faced, shaking his head. 'But you're Commander Blizzard,' he whispered. 'You as good as brought me up off the streets. I was your chosen man.'

Again, Voychek heaved a sigh. 'You know, I did have quite high hopes for you, Fletcher, but I give you one simple task to do and you bungle it.'

Fletcher glanced over to Dakkar. 'I didn't know, Dax. If I'd known he was Voychek, I'd 'ave never done it. He told me it was to keep you safe. He said there was great danger and that if I didn't do it, he'd hang me.'

'You have a choice now, though, Fletcher,' Voychek said. 'I am merciful. You can prove yourself to me now and I'll let you back into my ranks. You can become a captain of Cryptos.'

Fletcher blinked away his tears. 'Really?' he stammered, licking his lips. 'You . . . you'd let me off?'

Voychek held out a dagger. 'Cut the prince's throat,' he said. 'And prove you're worthy to serve Cryptos.'

Fletcher looked at the blade and then at Dakkar. 'Yes,' he said. 'What have I got to lose?' He took the dagger and strode towards Dakkar.

'Fletcher, think what you're doing!' Dakkar yelled.

'I know exactly what I'm doing, mate,' Fletcher growled. He grabbed Dakkar roughly by the hair and pulled his head back. 'You still got that flare handy?' he whispered into Dakkar's ear, sliding the dagger through his ropes.

A pistol shot cracked across the deck and Fletcher gave a scream of agony. Blood sprayed from his shoulder and he staggered towards the side of the ship, leaning heavily against the gunwales.

'You idiot,' Voychek said and leapt forward. With one fluid motion, he grabbed Fletcher's leg and upended him over the side. Fletcher's short scream ended in a splash.

Dakkar sprang free and plunged the fuse of the flare into a storm lantern, making it spark to life.

'Explosives wouldn't be a good idea here, Dakkar,' Voychek said, waving his hands towards the powder kegs and cannonballs. 'Each of these cannonballs is hollow, packed with the poisonous liquid mixture taken from the giant scorpions. If you blow up the ship, you know that the city would be enveloped in a cloud of lethal gas.'

Dakkar looked dismayed. 'I'd better get rid of it, then,' he said, hurling the flare over the side after Fletcher. It plopped into the water and he saw the fizzling red light sink into the depths.

Let's hope Georgia saw the signal, he thought. But when he turned, Voychek's sword nicked the skin of his neck.

'Admit it, Prince Dakkar,' Voychek said. 'You have met your match. One by one you have snuffed out my brothers, but it is I who will finish you off. And then I will take control of this island nation.'

'You're going to do that with an unruly mob outside Westminster?' Dakkar said, desperate to buy more time. He noticed Tegen stoop to pick up the dropped dagger behind Voychek with her bound hands.

'Always one step behind, my prince,' Voychek sneered. 'Once the riot reaches full height, I will bombard the Palace of Westminster with poison gas. Rebels, witnesses and the government will die in the toxic cloud.'

'But the King . . .'

'The King is insane, hidden away from the public in his castle, and his son and heir can easily be manipulated,' Voychek murmured. 'Or replaced. You'd be surprised how many spies and puppets Commander Blizzard has at his fingertips.'

'It'll never happen,' Dakkar said, straining his ears above the bustle on deck and the roar of anger on the shore, desperate to hear the whine of the *Nautilus*'s engine. Tegen slid back into the shadows. Dakkar could see her struggling to manipulate the dagger behind her back.

'You think not,' Voychek said, amused at Dakkar's bravado. 'When the mob is despatched and the government destroyed, who will step up to save the day? Why, noble Commander Blizzard. I'll declare martial law. The armies of Cryptos will be in charge. Britain is on the edge of a new era, Dakkar; it is poised to spread its power and influence across the globe. Britannia will rule the waves, Cryptos will rule Britannia and I will rule Cryptos!'

Tegen was sawing awkwardly through her bonds as crewmen hurried about, seemingly oblivious to the fact that she was trying to escape.

'I'll stop you!'

'You had your chance, Dakkar,' Voychek said, keeping the sword level with Dakkar's throat. 'If you had arrived a few minutes earlier, you would have caught us unloading the *Serqet*'s deadly cargo. You took longer than I anticipated to kill my brother, though.'

Dakkar thought about how unhappy Blizzard had been to see him when they sank the *Serqet*. It made more sense now. 'You knew I was in Algeria?'

Voychek laughed and lowered his sword a little. 'It's been my little game,' he whispered, his eyes gleaming. 'Setting you against my brothers in the sure and certain knowledge that you'd destroy them. I cooperated with Marek, allowed him to manufacture the poison gas, made him think we were partners. Then I encouraged his little plan to frame you and to lure you to him, knowing that his fate was sealed. You are an angel of death as far as Oginskis are concerned.'

Tegen's arms came free and she almost dropped the dagger. She pressed a finger to her lips.

'I'm here now,' Dakkar said, trying to keep Voychek's attention. 'Aren't you even a little worried?'

'Guns ready, sir!' bellowed a bald-headed marine, holding a flaming torch.

Voychek gave a sly grin. 'No, because it all ends now . . .'

At that moment, Tegen leapt at Voychek, the dagger flashing in the torchlight. At the same time, a huge BOOM shuddered through the groaning timbers of HMS *Slaughter*. Everyone on board fell as the deck tilted, sending cannons sliding back.

Tegen rolled away from her target, leaving the dagger embedded in his shoulder. Voychek scrambled to his feet almost immediately and tore the blade out of his flesh with an infuriated yell. Men screamed as barrels and cannon rolled over them and rigging fell from above, burying marines and sailors alike.

Voychek's face contorted into a mask of rage. 'What have you done?' he said through clenched teeth.

'That was no explosive I threw away before. It was the signal flare for Georgia to ram the ship. HMS *Slaughter* is going down and you're going with her!'

CHAPTER THIRTY-ONE
VENGEANCE

'So you think you've won, eh? Who do you think benefitted most from the demise of the Blizzard family, Prince Dakkar?' he sneered as he pulled a pistol from his belt. 'You and your precious mentor, Franciszek! Just think: he lived and slept in that castle knowing that fish picked the flesh from the bones of the previous owners at the foot of that cliff!' Voychek fired the shot and, instinctively, Dakkar ducked. But the bullet wasn't meant for Dakkar. He turned to see Tegen falling.

Dakkar ran to catch her. 'Tegen!'

'Foolish woman.' Voychek growled, 'I should have taken care of her many years ago. Now it's your word against mine about my identity, Dakkar, and you're already wanted for murder.'

Voychek laughed and hurried towards his cabin, leaving Dakkar holding the gasping Tegen. He looked down at her helplessly.

'Don't let him get away with it,' she said through gritted teeth. 'Stop him. Avenge my family. Avenge the Blizzards!' Her face creased with pain and her eyes closed.

Dakkar lay her gently on the deck and stood up. Water lapped around his feet as the ship sank.

'Voychek!' he yelled. 'Come out and face me! For today either you or I or both of us go down with this ship!'

As if in reply, two muted bangs echoed from the rear of the ship. A sheet of brilliant white silk billowed up and formed a balloon that rose in the air. Dakkar's eyes widened as a small part of the stern of the ship followed the balloon. Voychek stood on the platform, gripping the tight ropes that joined the balloon to the raft. He looked weak and his shirt dripped red where Tegen had stabbed him. 'It'll have to be just you then, my prince,' he shouted hoarsely, and gave a mocking salute. 'I'm so glad I was able to harvest all the inventions my brothers used once you'd sent them to hell! Now their combined ingenuity will ensure that I, the last, the only Oginski fit to rule, will triumph!'

'No!' Dakkar snarled and ran forward, clambering up the steps to the poop deck and sprinting to the side. The ship was sinking fast and the water dragged at Dakkar, slowing him down. He ran across the deck and leapt on to the gunwale, launching himself into the air. It was Voychek's turn to look amazed as Dakkar drew level with the rising platform and grabbed the ropes, pulling himself on board and kicking out at Voychek as he landed. Voychek staggered back to the edge of the platform and fell to the floor.

'How could you do that?' Dakkar snarled. 'How could you treat life so casually?'

Voychek snorted and clambered to his feet, drawing a sword as he did so. 'And you haven't? You never thought about the men who died in all the destruction you caused? You are as much of a killing machine as I am, Dakkar.'

'But to kill a whole family and take their name,' Dakkar gasped. 'To gas and poison innocent men and women . . .' He drew his own sword and stood, ready for Voychek's attack.

'You know the arguments by now, Dakkar,' Voychek said, panting hard and circling around him. 'Cryptos was never a slick organisation with a plan and a clear leadership. It was more an association of maniacs who happen to be related by blood. I am merely bringing order to that chaos.'

Dakkar attempted an exploratory jab with his sword but it was knocked aside. 'Order?' he said. 'You call this order?'

'My brothers would never have cooperated fully with each other,' Voychek said, slashing down with his sword, sending a numbing pain through Dakkar's sword arm. 'The world is carved up between squabbling, petty families already, but I will bring it under the rule of one leader.'

'You tricked your own brothers into fighting with each other just to profit from it?' Dakkar snapped, crushing the flat of his sword against Voychek's and coming close to him.

'Some needed less persuasion than others.' Voychek grinned, blood trickling from his mouth. 'Marek never knew that most of his men worked for me. That he was making the secret weapon that would bring me to power.'

'The captain of the *Serqet* was playing both of you against each other,' Dakkar said, trying to taunt Voychek.

Voychek sneered. 'That fool would have been the first to die in the bombardment. I sent him to clear a path for my marines when we landed.'

Dakkar threw Voychek back; he could see the sweat on his face. Clearly the man had lost a lot of blood. 'But what about Project Nemo?'

'A stroke of genius,' Voychek said, grinning and parrying another blow. 'Using my brothers as the external threat, I, as the safe, reliable Commander Blizzard, persuaded the government to fund a Cryptos faction within its own borders . . .'

Dakkar stabbed again, forcing Voychek back. 'Project Nemo.'

'I used the power and wealth of the United Kingdom to hunt down my own brothers and build my own army,' Voychek panted. 'And using you when the occasion suited, while poor, dear Franciszek trained you and fed you and kept you ready for the next adventure.'

'And then you let him die when he was no longer of any use,' Dakkar said, jagging his blade through the sleeve of Voychek's jacket and drawing blood.

Voychek winced and pulled back, making a few feints

with his sword. 'I wasn't present when that happened,' Voychek said. '*You* let him fall, I believe. . .'

'No!' Dakkar shouted. Blood pulsed in his ears as he hacked again and again at Voychek, who desperately held his blade up, trying to parry the blows.

'Didn't your precious mentor ever tell you to control your evil temper?' Voychek said and swung his hooked hand round, tearing at Dakkar's stomach.

Pain seared through Dakkar's guts and he fell to the floor. Voychek brought his knee up to Dakkar's head and stars flashed before his eyes as he keeled sideways.

'You are weak,' Voychek said softly as he stood over Dakkar. The man looked paler than ever, the red blood in stark contrast with his white skin. He looked feverish from the wound and the effort of fighting. 'You're too soft, too full of concern for those too feeble to stand on their own two feet. And you have fulfilled your purpose. What to do? That's the question. Hand you in for hanging? Pin the blame for all of this on you? No. I doubt you'd keep quiet, and it would look a bit odd if I ripped your tongue out.' Voychek gave a sigh. 'No, it looks as if you'll have to die here. Now.'

CHAPTER THIRTY-TWO
FRIENDS AND FORGIVENESS

Dakkar lay helpless, doubled up in pain from the gash Voychek had inflicted. He felt as though he'd been gutted. Voychek gave him a kick that sent him rolling to the edge of the platform. He looked down to see HMS *Slaughter* listing to the bottom of the Thames. Flotsam and wreckage swirled around as men clung on to it for dear life. He thought about poor Tegen, bleeding on the deck, and Fletcher, thrown to his death.

The *Nautilus* bobbed beneath them; it had surfaced and Dakkar could see Georgia standing on the tower. *It'd be nice to sail beneath the waves one more time*, he thought. *To escape the horrible betrayals and back-stabbing of the world.*

'It really has been an entertainment working with you,' Voychek said, raising his sword. 'But you've outstayed your welcome. I'm afraid this Oginski is a little harder to kill than the others.'

Dakkar frowned. He could see Georgia so clearly, and she had a rifle held to her shoulder. *She's the best shot of the two of us*, he thought with a smile.

'I'm so much . . . stronger than . . . you,' Dakkar croaked. 'Do you know why?'

Voychek snorted. 'Enlighten me,' he said.

'Because I have friends,' Dakkar whispered, rolling his eyes towards the *Nautilus*.

The distant crack of Georgia's rifle sounded far below them. Voychek gave a strangled cry as a bullet pierced his body. A flower of blood blossomed around the blackened hole that had just appeared in the chest of his tunic.

'You might be right,' he said, staring down at Dakkar. The light went from his pale eyes and he toppled forward on to him. Dakkar rolled aside in time to let Voychek's lifeless body tumble down into the Thames.

Another rifle crack split the air and he became aware of a rent in one of the balloons. Gradually the platform began to sink and Dakkar closed his eyes, letting consciousness slip away. He was safe.

Georgia's face blurred into focus, and Dakkar realised he lay in the control room of the *Nautilus*. 'I'm getting a bit sick of pulling you out of the water, young man,' she said, smiling gently.

Ibrahim's face appeared beside hers. 'Is he alive?' he said. 'Are you alive, your highness?'

Dakkar winced as he sat up, touching the fresh white bandages that wrapped his stomach. 'Yes, I'm very much alive,' he said. 'My head aches, my body aches and I feel as if I've been trampled by horses, but I'm alive.'

'Glad to hear it, Dakkar,' said Fletcher from the back of the tower. Dakkar glared at him. The boy was free, dressed in dry clothes. He had his arm in a sling and a bandage around his head.

'I saw him go over the side and risked pulling him out of the water. I couldn't leave him to drown, Dakkar,' Georgia said, her face pinched and pale. 'He was scared and didn't know what to do.'

'Blizzard . . .' Fletcher stopped and corrected himself. 'Voychek brought me up off the streets. I respected him. When he told me to disable the *Nautilus*, I didn't know what to do. I was terrified. I thought he wanted to keep you out of danger. I didn't know he was Voychek, honestly, Dakkar! And I didn't know he was going to send those horrible things after us. If I had known, I'd have never done it. You're my friends.'

Dakkar sighed. 'The one thing the Oginski brothers couldn't do was forgive,' he said. 'Virtually everyone I know has betrayed me in some way. I don't know who to trust.'

'You can trust me,' Fletcher said. 'Honest, Dakkar. I won't let you down again.'

'I'm not sure I can trust you, Fletcher, but I can forgive,' Dakkar said, giving a tight smile. 'Maybe in time. You did cut me free, after all.'

'Well, you've got your wish,' Georgia said.

Dakkar frowned. 'What do you mean?'

'I sent Ibrahim ashore on a little scouting mission,' Georgia said. 'The rioting has been stopped. The rumour is that revolutionaries took HMS *Slaughter* but Blizzard scuppered her before she could be used against the King. We could send a letter to James Clark-Ross, explaining everything, but for now you, it seems, died trying to help Blizzard. You're a dead man. Free to roam where you want. Nobody . . .'

'Nemo,' Dakkar said.

'Prince Nemo,' Ibrahim said, making a low bow.

Dakkar shook his head. 'No,' he said. 'Captain Nemo.'

'So should we send the letter?' Georgia asked, raising her eyebrows.

'I don't think so,' Dakkar said.

'Then where to now, Captain Nemo?' Georgia asked.

'Who knows?' Dakkar said. 'The seas are wide and deep. Let's go and see what adventures we find beneath them!'

'Yes, it has come to an end, and a better end than might have been expected after so many adventures!'

Jules Verne, *César Cascabel*

A NOTE FROM THE AUTHOR

CAPTAIN NEMO

This book brings Prince Dakkar face to face with the person he will become in later life: Captain Nemo. In the books by Jules Verne, Nemo is distrustful and quick to anger. He lives beneath the waves, avoiding mankind. I always thought that Nemo must have been badly let down by people he admired to be so cautious of strangers, and that is what I wanted to show.

GIANT INSECTS

Some insects grew to epic proportions in prehistoric times, possibly due to a more oxygen-rich atmosphere. My giant insects are a bit exaggerated but I hope that added to the fun. I have to admit that creepy-crawlies are definitely not my thing, so writing this has had me squirming in my seat sometimes!

HISTORICAL NOTES

The explosion of Mount Tambora in 1815 threw tons of volcanic ash into the atmosphere and created in 1816 what came to be known as the Year Without Summer. Crops failed and famine swept the land. 1816 was also the year that, trapped inside by torrential rain, Mary Shelley thought up the story of Frankenstein and his monster.

There was no actual rioting in London in 1816, but with soldiers returning from the Napoleonic wars and crops failing, fear of revolution was very real. The Pentrich Uprising took place in 1817 in Derbyshire and is sometimes known as England's last revolution. Two years later, in 1819, hundreds of protestors were injured and many killed in the Peterloo Massacre in Manchester.

Algiers was a centre for piracy and a base for the Barbary pirates for many centuries up until the mid 1800s. Pirates did roam the coasts of England and there are accounts of whole villages being taken away as slaves. The problem of piracy became so bad that Britain launched an attack on Algiers in August 1816, just after Dakkar's arrival there. The Dey of Algiers freed some 3,000 slaves and paid back all the ransom money taken. But piracy soon returned to the Mediterranean and beyond.

James Clark-Ross is a real historical figure who later became a famous naval officer and Arctic explorer. In my mind, Fletcher is a son of Fletcher Christian, the leader of the famous mutiny on HMS *Bounty*. It is said he died around 1793 on Pitcairn Island but legends persist that suggest he secretly returned to England. I thought it would be interesting to have that background for him, even though it is never mentioned!

Don't miss Dakkar's other adventures

 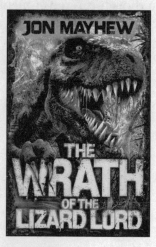

AVAILABLE NOW